The Color of Melancholy

Volume 1

Lynn R. Squire

Dedication

This book is dedicated to those who feel strongly about the emotions of others in a way they cannot explain and wish to understand them, as well as themselves, a bit more clearly.

And to those who wish to understand more about how emotions influence and envelope our lives through the essence we project to the world.

Acknowledgment

This book was completed after many years of contemplation on my own sensitivity to emotion and how best to express this sentiment to others. Through the encouragement of my family, I finally took upon myself the task of writing these books that I hope will resonate with others like me and those who are curious about how emotional vibes influence those around us.

I am grateful to those who helped to edit, publish, and revise this work and the many hours it took to get it to where we all felt comfortable.

I am most grateful to you, the reader, for giving this book a chance. I sincerely hope you find it engaging, educational, and helpful in understanding how we all struggle with an internal mosaic of emotions that project to others and how by understanding ourselves and seeing others in the same struggle, we can all help, lift, and love a little more along our journey.

About the Author

Lynn R. Squire is the author of various books on different topics like project management, a children's series on overcoming your fear of new or hard things, and, of course, this book, which attempts to explain how emotions are like radiant light that surrounds us and how darkness and melancholy can steal that light if left unresolved and unshared.

Lynn has always been interested in emotional health and learning productive ways to deal with his own depression, ADHD, and anxiety while being raised in a time that didn't recognize these challenges but brushed them aside as weaknesses or deficiencies.

Lynn has been married for many years and has numerous grandchildren living in the Mountain West. They provide him with health, healing, and joy every day, and they are the inspiration for writing this book.

Lynn works as a freelance project/program manager, IT consultant, scrum master, and small business marketing consultant and writes on the side for a creative release and out of a desire to be useful to others.

Preface

In a world that embraces the quiet truth of "each to his own," Ash stands apart. From a young age, he sensed that he perceived reality through a different lens—a lens that revealed the unspeakable sorrows and hidden burdens carried by those around him. While other children laughed and played, blissfully unaware of life's deeper struggles, Ash bore a weight that felt heavy and foreign, a burden never intended for him.

Instead of being crushed beneath the intensity of his empathy—the sorrow, the anger, the desperation of strangers pressing in on him like a second skin—he found a way to endure. Like a resilient flower weathering a storm, battered by the elements yet unwavering in its resolve to grow, Ash adapted to his circumstances. He learned to navigate a world overflowing with emotion, striving not just to survive but to truly live.

Now, standing at the crossroads of his life, Ash yearns to carve out a space that is solely his—a sanctuary from the relentless tide of others' feelings that surrounds him. He believes that perhaps by harnessing his gift to help those in need, he might lighten his own load and uncover meaning in his suffering.

Yet, life is rarely that straightforward. In this complex dance of light and shadow, Ash discovers that for every life he touches, there are those who seek to exploit his abilities for darker purposes. His journey becomes one of navigating the complex terrain where resilience meets sacrifice, where the will to stand firm is tested against a backdrop of crumbling foundations.

This is more than just a hero's story; it is a testament to the internal battles that shape us. For true courage does not always manifest in grand gestures. Sometimes, the fiercest struggles are fought in silence, away from the scrutiny of the world. For Ash, the greatest challenge he faces will stem not from an external adversary but from the relentless force threatening to engulf him from within.

As you turn these pages, join him on a journey of discovery, resilience, and the quest for identity against the tide of others' emotions.

Contents

Chapter 1: Glimmers of Light

Golden motes of dust danced lazily in the sunlight, slipping through the Star Wars curtains, their soft glow casting playful patterns across the walls. Outside, the muted chirp of sparrows blended with the distant hum of a waking world, calm and unhurried.

The floor unfurled as a chaotic treasure map of Ashton "Ash" Winters' imagination—strewn with toys, loose crayons, and the stray caps of markers. By the bed, a tower of books leaned precariously like a daring adventurer braving the pull of gravity, their dog-eared pages and glossy covers whispering of lands yet explored.

The walls told their own stories, vibrant and alive with Ash's dreams. A meadow teemed with butterflies, their wings captured mid-flight in bold swirls of color, stretching beneath a sky that melted from lavender to gold. Across another wall, a pirate ship sliced through a fiery red horizon, its sails puffed with unseen winds. But the centerpiece was unmistakable—a luminous figure painted with careful, deliberate strokes. Its warm light seemed to ripple out into the room, even when the curtains were drawn. The figure's hand extended outward, fingers grasping toward an unseen horizon, a secret promise or a dream just beyond reach.

Ash stirred beneath the blanket's rumpled folds, his auburn hair tousled into wild peaks that spoke of restless dreaming. His eyes fluttered open, slow and unfocused, before landing on the glowing figure that had watched over him through the night.

Ash was 11, but the world saw him differently. While most kids his age chased noise and screens, he lingered in stillness, treasuring the quiet places where stories could grow. His room was more than a bedroom to him—it was his refuge, his canvas, and the uncharted map of all the wonders waiting inside his mind.

Beyond the quiet walls of his room, he could hear the familiar rhythm of the morning unfolding. His mother's gentle voice drifted down the hall as she tried to wake Lily— an effort that was rarely met with immediate success. At nine years old, Lily had perfected the art of squeezing out every last second of sleep, stubbornly burrowing deeper into her blankets until she could no longer ignore the pull of the day.

Then, like clockwork, the shift happened. One moment, silence. The next was a burst of energy.

Soft footsteps turned into hurried ones, drawers opened and shut, and soon enough, Lily's voice filled the house. She spoke with a brightness that was impossible to ignore, humming absentmindedly as she moved through the hall. It wasn't long before Ash could hear her in the kitchen, chatting easily with their dad, her laughter weaving into the morning like sunlight streaming through the windows.

Ash found himself smiling. No matter how much she grew, Lily still carried that same warmth, the kind that made even the simplest mornings feel lighter. He could still remember her at seven years old, bouncing around the kitchen and singing songs about bunnies, her joy so infectious it was impossible not to join in.

But then, the sound of heavier footsteps reached his ears—slow, deliberate, and grounded. Ash didn't need to look to know who it was; he could tell it was his father, John Winters, making his way down the hall toward his room. His steps were solid and steady, the kind of quiet strength Ash admired.

Chuckling to himself, Ash rolled over and pulled the blanket tighter around him. Sure enough, the door creaked open, and Ash struggled to hold back his laughter, but he failed to completely stop moving.

"Oh no, you don't, buddy. I saw you," his father's voice rumbled from the doorway, feigning seriousness.

Before Ash could react, his father, John Winters, reached in and launched a surprise tickle attack through the blanket. The room filled with Ash's breathless giggles as he squirmed, trying to escape the relentless tickles. "Okay, okay! You got me!" Ash laughed, tossing the blanket aside in surrender.

As the laughter faded, Ash blinked at his father, still catching his breath. There, in front of him, stood John's familiar, weathered face, the corners of his mouth lifting into one of his rare but warm smiles. Ash noticed, as he always did, the soft golden glow that lingered around him—faint but unmistakable. It shimmered like light captured in the air, and for reasons Ash couldn't explain, it felt like something only he could see. It was comforting but a little strange, too.

John ruffled Ash's already tousled hair. "Time to get up and get ready for school, bud."

Ash nodded, sitting up slowly as his father turned to leave. John wasn't one for many words. He was someone who made an effort, someone who had built his own small electrician business. His love and care were often shown through his actions—working long hours to provide for them, making sure they had everything they needed—even if that meant he wasn't always around. But when he did show affection, in moments like this, it felt like the world paused for just a second, like nothing else mattered but this small connection.

Stretching his arms high above his head, Ash let out a soft yawn, the excitement for the first day of school starting to boil within him. Swinging his legs over the edge of the bed, he padded over to his closet, pulling open the door to reveal the crisp new clothes his mother had picked out for him.

The outfit was laid out perfectly—a bright blue polo shirt, khaki shorts, and a pair of sneakers that still smelled faintly of rubber. Ash grinned, running his fingers over the fabric. New clothes always carried a sense of possibility, as if wearing them made him a little braver and more ready for whatever adventures awaited.

But before long, his mind wandered. He picked up a sock, staring at it for a moment before his imagination took over.

In his mind's eye, the sock transformed into a fire-breathing dragon, its scaled body coiling around the villains threatening a fantastical kingdom. Ash stood triumphant, commanding the mighty creature as it roared, flames shooting through the air to vanquish his foes.

"Take that, you villains!" he muttered under his breath, swinging his arm in an imaginary strike.

A sudden voice snapped him back to reality. "Ash, you are late!"

Ash spun around to see his mother, Debra Winters, standing in the doorway, hands on her hips, exasperation and amusement coloring her face. The soft yellow haze Ash often noticed around her seemed to shimmer as she moved, adding an extra layer of warmth to her presence. As always, her voice rose dramatically as if it were the most serious situation in the world.

"Uh-oh!" Ash's voice rose into a theatrical as he realized he might actually be in trouble.

Debra, Ash's mother, was a force of nature. As a music teacher at the local elementary school, she spent her days orchestrating harmony among energetic students. Commanding yet warm, she had mastered the art of managing chaos in the classroom or at home.

She strode into the room with the precision of someone used to managing a classroom full of kids, "Ten minutes, Ash! What were you doing? Never mind, don't answer that.

We need to move!" She picked up his shirt and shorts, holding them out.

"Mom, I can do it myself!" Ash protested, his cheeks flushing with embarrassment.

"Yes, I can see that," she replied, glancing pointedly at his room. "But we're out of time for you to play superhero this morning."

Before Ash could respond, Debra whisked him toward the bathroom, nudging him in front of the sink. In a blur of motions, she helped him wash his face and brush his teeth, ignoring his halfhearted attempts to wave her off.

"Mom, stop!" he groaned, spitting out toothpaste. "I got this!"

With a playful roll of her eyes, his Mom said, "And by the time you're done, the school year will already be over."

Ash couldn't help but laugh; his mother's fussing was oddly comfortable, no matter how unnecessary.

"There. Done," she said, brushing off her hands like she'd just had a major achievement. She placed her hands on his shoulders, meeting his eyes with a grin. "Now go grab your bag. Have your breakfast, and then go off to school with Dad."

Ash slid into his chair at the kitchen table, his nose catching the familiar aroma of freshly brewed coffee mingling with the sweet scent of chocolate cereal. His father, John, sat across from him, nursing the blackest cup of coffee imaginable. The steam curled upwards, matching the quiet, steady energy that always seemed to surround him.

John was in mid-conversation with Ash's younger sister, Lily, a bundle of energy who seemed to shine with her own special light. As she hummed softly to herself, the soft pink shimmer that Ash always noticed around her grew slightly more vivid as if her happiness was spilling over.

When Lily spotted Ash, her face lit up. "Ash! Look!" she exclaimed, holding up her plate where John had arranged her pancakes into the shape of a bunny. "Dad shaped my pancakes into a bunny!"

Ash looked at the three circles, which had barely forged together to make a bunny shape, and pretended to be awed as he said, "That looks so cool, Lily."

John took a sip of his coffee, hiding his awkwardness behind the cup as he took a sip. "Yeah. That's a bunny."

Debra glanced at the pancakes, amused, "How about I try my hand at the bunny pancakes?"

She and John exchanged a look as he said, "Maybe next time. We are getting a little late."

Debra smiled as she turned away, her gaze falling on the piano. "If only I didn't have to go to work and Lily didn't have to go to school, we could have had a concert right here," Debra murmured wistfully as she zipped up Lily's lunchbox.

"Next time, Mom!" Lily chirped.

Ash, meanwhile, hurriedly spooned Cocoa Puffs into his bowl of milk, the cereal clinking against the sides. He shoveled the mix into his mouth as quickly as he could, his excitement about school battling with the time crunch.

When he finally looked up, his father was already gathering the dishes—his own, Lily's, and Ash's—stacking them neatly before carrying them to the sink. John's movements were remarkably efficient, and every step was purposeful.

"Let's go," John commanded, with a glance over his shoulder.

Ash hurried off his chair, grabbed his backpack, and slung it over one shoulder. Lily walked beside him with her pink Barbie bag while their mother locked the door of the house behind them, her floral embroidered bag in hand as she hid the key under the flower pot.

John held the car door open while Ash clambered into his seat, followed by Lily, who sat her bag on her lap. Their mother, Debra, slid into the passenger seat, giving the kids a quick, sweeping look as if ensuring they were perfectly presentable. John made quick work of strapping them in, his hands steady and practiced.

As soon as John took the driver's seat, the engine thrummed to life, and the familiar hum of their car filled the air. Lily began humming another song as Ash sat quietly, keenly interested in the view from his window.

It wasn't long before they pulled up in front of Ash's school. John slowed the car, glancing back at him in the rearview mirror. "Your stop's here, bud."

Debra turned in her seat, eyeing Ash with her usual motherly concern. "Do you need help getting off?"

Ash's eyes widened as he wrestled with his seatbelt, "No, no! It's okay, Mom. I got it!" The last thing Ash wanted was for his mom to hop out and start fussing over him in front of his classmates. That would be pure torture.

Debra remained in her seat, even though she was unconvinced.

Finally, Ash unbuckled his seatbelt and was just about to get out of the car when Lily leaned over, her eyes bright with mischief.

"Bye, Ash! Try not to be too grumpy today," she teased, giving him an exaggerated wave.

Ash huffed a laugh, ruffling her hair. "Yeah, yeah. You try not to take over the whole classroom."

"I make no promises," she shot back with a grin.

Shaking his head, Ash grabbed his backpack and slid out of the car, Lily's laughter following him as he shut the door.

"Bye, sweetheart!" Debra called after him, her voice tinged with pride.

John gave him a small wave, a hint of a smirk on his face. "Have a good one, kid."

Ash turned back as he reached the curb, waving at his family. The car lingered for a moment before pulling away, with Lily's voice still carrying through the open window as she sang her endless goodbye song. Ash shook his head, chuckling to himself as he turned to face the school building.

His heart lightened as he spotted his friends standing in a cluster near the school gates, their laughter and animated chatter reaching him even at a distance. It was a reassuring sight; despite the new term, the group dynamic hadn't shifted in the slightest. Silently thanking God for small mercies, Ash quickened his pace, the straps of his backpack bouncing against his shoulders. As he approached, something subtle yet familiar caught his eye—a faint shimmer of colors around his friends. It reminded him of the soft hues he often noticed around his parents.

Ever since he first became aware of these splashes of color, Ash had been curious about them. He had tried asking his parents, teachers, and friends, but nearly everyone had dismissed it as a figment of his imagination. Since the colors appeared so faintly, Ash eventually began to blur them out of his mind, treating them as nothing more than fleeting tricks of the light.

"Hey, Ash!" one of his friends called, waving him over.

The train of his thought evaporated at once, replaced by the warmth of familiarity as he jogged the remaining distance. His friends greeted him with the usual mix of teasing and excitement, and soon, they were all crowded together, showing off their new sneakers.

"Check these out," Ash said, holding up a foot to display his pristine white kicks with a bold red stripe.

"Whoa! Those are awesome," one of his friends exclaimed, leaning closer to inspect them.

They soon launched into a spirited discussion about the new Marvel movie. But Ash couldn't join in; he had read the comic long before the film's release, but his friends always asked him not to spoil the plot—after all, the comic usually came out first, and they preferred experiencing the story on the big screen for themselves.

Once again, Ash couldn't help but notice the shimmering colors around his friends. He tried to push it aside, focusing instead on the thrill of the first day back and the promise of familiar routines. *They would fade away like they always did. Nothing to worry about—just another ordinary day*, he thought.

And sure enough, the pulsating colors around his friends began to fade as the energy of the morning settled. Miss Thompson entered the classroom, going over to stand in the front. Her presence commanded the chatter into the soft scratch of pencils and the steady hum of the air conditioning.

As Ash finished the first task Miss Thompson had given the class, his gaze drifted to her. A faint lavender haze surrounded her, curling around her like a soft mist. Unlike the fleeting colors around his friends, this one didn't shift or vanish—it lingered, steady and calm.

Ash leaned his chin on his hand, studying her. There was something different about the color that followed Miss Thompson. It felt alive, almost as if it was a part of her, carrying the same gentleness with which Miss Thompson conducted herself.

For the umpteenth time, he wondered if anyone else could see it and glanced around the room. His classmates were either focused on their work or sneaking glances at the clock—no one seemed to notice a thing.

Ash shifted uncomfortably in his seat. His mind was spinning with questions yet again—what were those colors? Why could he see them? Was it normal?

For now, though, he kept his thoughts to himself, letting Miss Thompson's faint lavender glow wash over him as he listened to her voice. Whatever these colors were, he suspected he would have plenty of time to figure it out.

***

Time passed, and the bell rang, signaling the end of the first day of school. Ash joined his friends on the bus, the familiar rhythm of their jokes and stories helping him forget about the soft glimmers he had seen in the morning.

When the school bus stopped in front of Ash's house, he waved goodbye to his friends and got off. Trudging up the driveway, he crouched down to retrieve the spare key hidden under a potted plant, a trick his parents had taught him last year. After struggling for a moment, he finally managed to unlock the door, and it creaked open.

Peering into the silence, Ash called out, "Mom? Dad? Lily? Is anyone home?"

But no one called back.

Ash frowned, worried that his mom and Lily weren't home yet. They usually arrived by the time he got back. He recalled his father once telling him, "Ash, if your mom and I aren't back by the time you are, head to your friend Leon's house, okay?"

Ash was about to turn to do exactly that when something caught his eye. The bag his Mom had taken to school that day sat on the kitchen table—she had to be home.

"Mom?" Ash called again.

Hearing a faint creak from the floorboard upstairs made him freeze. Setting his backpack down by the door, Ash slowly made his way upstairs. Reaching the top, he noticed the door to his parents' bedroom was slightly ajar. Pushing it open gently, Ash peered inside.

The room was dark as the lights had been kept turned off. But Ash knew that the figure who sat on the edge of the bed with their shoulders hunched was no one other than his mother. She seemed so different from her usual self. A smoky haze lingered around her, making it seem as if she was a part of the darkness in the room.

Ash whispered, trying not to startle his mother, "Mom?"

Despite trying his best, his mother seemed startled as she tried to wipe her eyes hidden from him, "Ash, sweetie. You're back already? I must've lost track of time."

Ash stepped closer but was still unsure as he asked, "Are you okay?"

Although his mother forced a smile, it didn't quite reach her eyes. "I'm fine, honey. Why don't you go downstairs and start your homework? I'll be down in a bit."

Ash nodded slowly, even though he didn't want to leave. The haze was unlike anything he had seen until now. It couldn't be a trick of the light, and it couldn't be his mere imagination. It was definitely real—and for the first time, he wasn't all too willing to brush it aside.

Chapter 2: First Flashes

The next day, Miss Thompson tried rather unsuccessfully to teach him and his classmates, for there was hardly any energy in the classroom. Most students appeared to be drifting off, their eyes focusing anywhere but on the board, while some fiddled with their pencils.

"Class," she said, cutting through the fog of inattentiveness, "let's refocus. Fractions are important! You'll need these skills when you're baking cookies or calculating how much allowance you've saved for that video game."

A few heads turned briefly but most quickly returned to their own distractions. Ash glanced at her and then down at his desk, his pencil aimlessly tapping against the worksheet in front of him.

"Ash Winters," Miss Thompson's voice sharpened as she zeroed in on him. "Can you simplify three-fourths multiplied by two-thirds?"

Startled, Ash blinked and stammered, "Uh… one-half?"

Her eyebrows raised, though her tone remained patient. "Close, but not quite. Let's try again—multiply the numerators and the denominators."

"Six-twelfths?" he guessed.

"Which simplifies to…?"

Ash hesitated. "One-half?"

"There you go!" she said, though there was a faint sigh in her voice. "Now, let's try to stay with the class, shall we?"

"Sorry, Miss Thompson," Ash mumbled, but his focus quickly drifted again. No matter how hard he tried, his thoughts kept circling back to yesterday, gnawing at the edges of his mind like a persistent echo.

The smoky haze that had surrounded his mother the day before was nothing like the soft, warm yellow glow he was used to seeing around her. That glow felt like home, like comfort. But the haze yesterday? It slithered and coiled like a snake, leaving him feeling uneasy.

It had gnawed at him so much that he could barely sleep last night. Every time he closed his eyes, the image of that haze returned, darker and heavier, as if it were pressing down on him. He tossed and turned, his sheets a tangled mess by the time the clock struck midnight. The unease lingered no matter how much he tried to convince himself it was nothing.

The murmur of voices behind him broke through his fog of thoughts. Kevin and Jamie were whispering animatedly, their conversation just loud enough for Ash to catch snippets.

"...like when he gets angry, he's unstoppable," Jamie was saying.

"Yeah, but that's the thing," Kevin replied. "Most of the time, he's just chill, so he gets his butt kicked. It's only when he's mad that his power shows up."

Ash's ears perked up, and he focused completely on the conversation behind him, even though his eyes remained on Miss Thompson.

Angry.

The word stuck in Ash's mind, circling like a buzzing fly. He looked at Miss Thompson, who was explaining something about equivalent fractions, her steady lavender aura pulsing faintly around her. It was soft and calm, much like her usual demeanor—collected and patient, even when she was frustrated.

But then it happened.

Her aura flickered, a faint ripple that matched the crease forming between her brows as she frowned at the classroom's lack of focus. The shift was subtle, but Ash noticed it.

Could it be...?

Something clicked inside him, a thought that hadn't crossed his mind before. Maybe the changes in the colors he observed weren't random. What if they had something to do with emotions?

It wasn't a definite conclusion—more like the beginnings of a hypothesis. He leaned back slightly, his mind racing. If emotions could trigger changes in those auras, it might explain the smoky haze surrounding his mother. She had been tense and hurried yesterday, maybe even upset. Could that have caused the shift in her usual glow?

Ash's gaze fell to his desk, his thoughts swirling chaotically. If emotions were involved, then why had his mother been upset the other day? Or could the black haze he sensed be linked to a different feeling entirely? He furrowed his brow, recalling that his mother had been particularly upset when he had been late for school that morning.

Could that have been the reason?

The thought tightened his chest. He couldn't confirm it, but the possibility weighed heavily on him. He didn't want to be the cause of his mother's sadness, especially not the kind that could dim her usual warm glow and turn it into something unsettling, like that smoky haze.

I need to get my act together, he told himself, a wave of realization washing over him. He wouldn't be late for school again or anything else that mattered. If there was even the slightest chance that his actions could affect his mother's emotions—and, by extension, her glow—he needed to do better.

With renewed determination, Ash straightened in his chair and gripped his pencil—no more excuses, no more slip-ups.

****

When Ash entered his home, he was filled with a strong resolve to follow through with his plan. He was thrilled to see that his dad was home from work earlier than usual. Excited, Ash dashed toward him.

"Dad, you're home so early!" Ash exclaimed as he wrapped his arms tightly around his father in a hug.

John patted his son on the back, "Yeah, I got lucky today."

Ash was about to continue, perhaps asking about the early return, but as he stepped back, something caught his eye. His father's usual golden sheen, the steady and solid aura he was accustomed to, appeared in complete disarray. It flickered and swirled chaotically, a stark contrast to the neutral expression on John's face.

Ash hesitated, his excitement fading into unease. "Dad, are you okay?"

Surprised by the sudden concern in his son's voice, John replied, "I'm great, bud. Why do you ask? Did I do something to make you think otherwise?"

At his question, the gold color surrounding him seemed to churn even more, becoming increasingly unstable. Ash blinked, struggling to reconcile what he was seeing with his understanding of his father. Nothing in John's demeanor or tone suggested anything was wrong, yet the erratic shimmer around him told a different story.

Maybe I misunderstood, Ash thought. Perhaps the colors didn't mean what he assumed they did. For the first time in a long while, Ash felt an overwhelming urge to tell his father everything: About the colors, what they meant—or at least what he thought they meant. Maybe his dad could help him make sense of it all.

John was watching him closely now, waiting for Ash to say something. The room felt still, and for a moment, it seemed like Ash might actually go through with it. But just as he opened his mouth, the front door swung open, and Debra and Lily walked in.

"Hey, Ash, guess what?" Lily piped up, breaking the quiet. "Mr. Flopsy finally ate a carrot today! But he took so long that I swear I could've finished all my homework before he was done. Do you think rabbits get stomach aches if they eat too slowly? Or maybe they're just built differently?"

Ash tried to focus on her story about the classroom pet rabbit, Mr. Flopsy, but his attention was elsewhere. As his mom knelt down to pat a stray leaf off Lily's hair, something caught his eye.

The yellow glow around his mother now had something strange running through it—a faint, thread-like streak of purple.

Debra's tired expression struck Ash in particular, and the words he'd been holding back froze in his throat, silencing the urge to consult his dad. Now didn't feel like the right time to ask questions or share his strange secret.

Ash quieted down as the vibrant chatter of his family continued around him as if nothing had changed. That night, he tossed and turned in bed, unable to find the rest he desperately needed. His mother's glimmer, interlaced with that strange purple thread, played over and over in his mind. What did it mean? Was it tied to her emotions? Or worse, was it something he'd done? The thought was unbearable, and by the time he finally drifted off, the night was almost giving way to morning.

***

When his alarm blared the next day, Ash jolted awake, groggy and disoriented. Realizing how late it was, he scrambled to get dressed. His mind raced as he shoved on his clothes, barely registering the sounds of the house around him.

The door to his room suddenly flew open, and there stood his mother, hands on her hips.

"Ash Winters! Late. Again!" she snapped. The sharpness of her frustration cut through his morning haze. "How many times have I told you not to play in the morning? We simply don't have the time for it!"

Ash fumbled with his shirt, mumbling an apology. "But I wasn't playing—"

"No excuses, Ash," she interrupted, her tone firm. "Hurry up!"

She stepped in to help him button his shirt and smooth out his bedhead, her movements brisk and efficient. Ash stayed quiet, his gaze fixed on her. The buzzing purple flare within her usual yellow glow had grown more pronounced, almost like a volcano ready to erupt.

He wanted to say something, anything, but the words wouldn't come. Instead, he remained silent, watching her and the swirling colors around her, feeling small and powerless.

As John dropped Ash off at school, Ash noticed that the colors shimmering around his classmates had become more pronounced. Some were buzzing like the purple thread in his mother's yellow aura, while others were eerily quiet. It came across as a symphony of colors, overwhelming his senses and tightening his chest with anxiety.

Suddenly, he didn't feel like approaching his friends. Their colors seemed brighter and louder than usual, so he decided to avoid them. As he walked into the school, he could feel his friends' confused expressions following him. A few of them called out, "Ash!?" But he didn't look back.

By the time class started, the buzzing and pulsing of the colors had calmed down a little, but Ash still felt jittery, his nerves humming like a live wire. He tried to focus, but his mind kept circling back to his mother—how upset she had been that morning and how the purple in her aura had clashed with her yellow. He didn't want to make her upset. He didn't want to be the reason the colors flickered like that.

By lunchtime, he hoped to have some peace, but it was anything but quiet. The hallway and cafeteria were filled with so much energy that the air itself seemed to vibrate with colors. The effect was so intense that it felt like it was drilling into his skull. His heart began racing, and the noise buzzing in his ears grew unbearable.

It was too much.

Ash felt an overwhelming urge to escape, to get away from the bright, flashing colors and the noise that seemed to follow him everywhere. His breath came in short bursts, and without thinking, he bolted. He pushed through the crowded hallway, ignoring the calls of his friends shouting after him, "Ash?! Where are you going?"

But he didn't care. He just needed to get away. His legs carried him past lockers and classrooms through the school to the nearest exit. His mind screamed at him to stop, but he couldn't. He needed somewhere quiet, somewhere dark, somewhere the buzzing would cease so his thoughts could finally settle. He wasn't paying attention to where he was going.

Suddenly, he crashed into something hard. His body flew backward, and before he could register what happened, he hit the ground with a sickening thud. Pain exploded in his skull, and everything around him blurred. His vision spun, making the world feel like it was tumbling, twisting, and turning at an impossible speed.

"Ah!" he gasped, his head spinning uncontrollably as his eyes fluttered open. He could barely make out Miss Thompson's face hovering above him, her expression filled with concern.

"Oh no, Ash! Are you okay?" she asked, worried.

Ash tried to speak, but all he could manage was to blink up at her as the world continued to spin around him. "Ms.

Thompson," he mumbled, "the world... it's just moving so fast. Why?"

Before Mrs. Thompson could respond, Ash's world darkened, finally granting him the peace he had been seeking so desperately.

***

Ash's eyes fluttered open, and his vision remained blurry for at least a moment or two before he could finally focus. He blinked again, feeling a sharp, stinging pain in his head. The world around him still seemed to spin, with persistent, vivid colors throbbing in his surroundings. As his eyes slowly adjusted, he saw his father sitting by his bedside, his face creased with concern.

"Dad?" Ash whispered.

John leaned in, asking gently, "Yes, buddy? How are you feeling?"

Ash swallowed, still pained, with ringing in his ears. He sensed a whirlwind of colors swirling around him, pulsating like an uncontrollable storm. The golden glow radiating from his father appeared brighter than usual, heightening the dizzying sensation.

"I'm tired," Ash murmured, his eyes drifting closed again. "When can we go home?"

John nodded. "Soon, bud. We've called the doctor. He said you have a concussion, but once he checks you and gives the okay, we can go home, alright?"

Ash barely nodded; his exhaustion felt too heavy to lift. "Promise?"

"I promise," John reassured him, brushing his hand through Ash's hair.

Ash closed his eyes again, trying to shut out the bright, buzzing colors. The world felt like it was pressing in on him, and all he wanted was to rest. Moments later, he sensed the doctor's presence nearby, the soft blue glow emanating from him as he checked Ash's eyes.

The doctor's gentle voice was a distant hum in Ash's mind. "Looks like you're doing okay now. No signs of anything more serious, but we'll need to take it easy for a bit. I'll clear you to go home, but no physical activities until you're feeling better."

John stood up, relieved. "Thank you, Doctor."

"Take care of him," the doctor said with a smile, patting John on the shoulder. "Get him some rest."

John turned back to Ash, lifting him gently and carrying him to the car. Ash barely registered the movement; his body felt heavy with fatigue. When they arrived home, John carefully carried Ash to his bed, laying him down as gently as possible.

For the first time in what felt like forever, Ash finally had the chance to sleep. The buzzing colors seemed to quiet as his eyelids fluttered shut, and he relaxed into the comforting embrace of his bed.

But suddenly, or so it seemed, the shrill ring of a phone cut through the stillness, pulling him from the comfort of his dreams. He opened his eyes, still feeling heavy, though the sensation was fleeting.

Slowly, Ash pushed himself up. His body ached from the lingering weariness of the concussion. Although his head still felt heavy, the strain in his father's voice from another room was enough to motivate him to move. He swung his legs off the bed; the cool floor beneath his feet helped ground him slightly.

Curiosity gnawed at him as he made his way toward the hallway. He paused before the slightly ajar door of his father's home office, where faint sounds of a conversation filtered through.

After hesitating for a moment, Ash pushed the door open just enough to peer inside.

"Ben, I told you to keep a strict watch over the newbies," his father's voice was filled with a tension Ash had never heard before. "How could you leave them alone?"

Ash blinked, trying to make sense of his father's words. Before he could grasp the full meaning, his father's voice rose, sharp with anger.

"The newbie did what?!"

The urgency in his father's tone sent a chill down Ash's spine. His heart began to pound faster in his chest.

"And where in the world were you?!"

He watched in stunned silence as the golden glow around his father, usually so steady and warm, instantly shifted. The vibrant hues swirled, crackling with energy. The comforting light Ash had always known now seemed to twist into something chaotic and violent.

"How could you just leave the newcomers alone?!"

Something the man on the other end said suddenly made John raise his phone and throw it against the wall. The phone broke into a million pieces, reflecting his aura, once calm and stable, flared into a searing red—fiery, volatile, and so intense that Ash felt it in his chest as if the very air had changed. His vision blurred, and the room around him seemed to swim as though the very space was shaking. He gasped for air, but the weight of the colors pressed down on him, making it harder to breathe. The red surrounding his father was so vivid and explosive that it felt suffocating.

Fear gripped Ash's chest. He stumbled back, his heart racing as the pressure of the red light seemed to close in on him. His father was angry—more than Ash had ever witnessed before. The sight of that violent, pulsing red glow terrified him, leaving him feeling small and utterly powerless.

Without thinking, Ash turned and fled, his feet moving before his mind could catch up. He ran back to his room, pulling the flimsy covers over his head; it was all he had. His hands trembled as he buried his face in the fabric, trying to block out everything—his father's anger, the intense colors, and their never-ending buzz.

Ash's heart raced in his chest. For the first time in his life, he felt afraid of the person who had always been his source of security. Everything he had known about his father seemed to have fractured at that moment. All that was left was the chaos of the red and the unbearable weight of the emotions that accompanied it.

Tears welled in Ash's eyes, not just from fear but from confusion. What was happening? Why was it happening to him? Did he cause it? Was he the reason the colors were so bright and loud? What was he supposed to do now? Who was he supposed to go to?

***

Hours passed, and Ash remained under the covers until he heard his mother, who had arrived home from work. Her voice tinged with a weariness that Ash was all too familiar with, carried through the hall.

"… Is Ash okay? Can I see him?"

Lily's voice was laced with concern, the little girl unaware of the deeper, more complicated storm raging in their home. Ash's heart squeezed, but before he could fully process the conversation, his mother's voice followed, laced with exhaustion.

"No can do, Lily. Ash is badly hurt, and he needs some rest today. I'll go see him right now, and you can see him tomorrow, okay?"

Ash curled up further under the covers, the comfort of the blanket doing little to alleviate the knot in his stomach. He wanted to call out to his mother, to tell her he was okay, but the overwhelming weight of his emotions—fear, confusion, and shame—kept him silent.

His mother's footsteps approached, and Ash could hear her soft sigh as she pushed open his door. The creak of the hinges felt too loud in the stillness of the room. Then his mother was there, pulling back the covers gently, her touch both comforting and intrusive.

"Ash, sweetheart," Debra said gently, but there was a clear edge of concern, "How are you feeling? I heard you got a concussion."

Ash winced as he sat up, his head spinning slightly. The pain from the fall was still there, but it paled in comparison to the dizziness that came from everything he was seeing. His hands shook as he ran them through his hair, and he tried to ignore the bright yellow glow that surrounded his mother, now tinged with something darker that he couldn't quite place.

"I—I'm fine," Ash mumbled, his voice weak and strained. "Just... just tired." He hesitated for a moment, unsure if he should say more. But the words he had been dying to speak felt like they were stuck in his throat.

"What were you thinking, running through the hallway like that?" Debra asked.

Ash took a deep breath, the words bubbling up in his throat. He needed to tell her. He had to, if only to explain what these strange colors and overwhelming sensations were. He looked up at his mother, her tired face waiting for him to speak, and he finally blurted out, "Mom, I—I've been seeing things. The colors... they're not normal. They—"

But before he could finish, Debra held up her hand, cutting him off with a soft, dismissive chuckle. "Ash, honey, you've got a concussion. You're probably just imagining things. You know how your mind works when you're not feeling well."

Ash's heart sank, and he felt a knot tighten in his chest. "But, Mom, it's not just in my head. I see them everywhere—people, the air—everything is glowing and changing. I don't know what it means, but it's real!" His voice shook, desperation evident as he tried to make her understand.

Debra brushed her hair back in mild frustration, and Ash could see her tired eyes darting away from his, her attention shifting. "Sweetheart," she said, her tone intended to be soothing but only making Ash feel smaller, "you've been through a lot today. You're probably just tired. You can't be thinking straight." She patted his hand gently as if trying to calm him, but the words stung. "Maybe you should rest now. I'm sure you'll feel better in the morning. And these... strange ideas? They'll go away once you're well."

Ash opened his mouth, but his words tangled in the realization that she wasn't hearing him. He watched his mother shift the conversation back to herself. "I don't know if I'm coming or going lately. I've got so much to deal with, and I swear, no one sees how hard I work. Your dad doesn't even want to talk to me, holed up in that office of his."

Ash sat there, watching his mother as she spoke, her one-sided conversation growing more distant. She wasn't seeing him; she wasn't hearing him. Frustration twisted inside him, but he didn't know how to make her understand or how to make her see what was happening to him. All he could think was that his mother was truly tired.

After a long pause, he finally whispered, "You work hard, Mom. You deserve rest."

"I won't disturb you any longer," he added, the words feeling inadequate, but they were all he had.

His mother didn't seem to hear him and nodded absently, caught up in her own thoughts. "Yes, I think I'll go and rest in my room now," she said, turning away and walking out of the room.

Ash lay back in his bed, his mind a jumble of emotions and questions. As his mother's yellow aura swirled out of the room, he noticed a thick grey haze outlining it—subtle at first but growing more pronounced as she walked away. It was hard to ignore, like a shadow distorting the bright energy around her. His heart sank.

It wasn't just his mother—Ms. Thompson's lavender glow and his father's golden one both had faint grey outlines, thin but present. The grey haze felt ominous as if something was slowly consuming the light.

Ash stared at the door, feeling a deep unease. Something was wrong, and it felt connected to him, but he couldn't understand why. The colors, once vibrant, now seemed to fade into something darker, leaving him lost in confusion.

What could he do to prevent all that was happening to him?

Chapter 3: Hidden Patterns

The shrill sound of the alarm beside his bed pierced the quiet of the early morning, pulling Ash out of a restless sleep. He groggily reached out, silencing it with a quick jab, and sat up. His eyes scanned the room, now foreign. Gone were the action figures of his favorite superheroes and racing cars. They had been replaced with a sanctuary of books, paints, and blank canvases. The only relics of the past were the walls, which still showed the marks of his early inventiveness.

With a sigh, Ash swung his legs off the bed and stood, stretching the sleep from his muscles. At fourteen, Ash's world had shifted from imaginary battles and fantastical dreams to an eye-opening reality. His mornings had become methodical. Wash up. Brush his teeth. Wake Lily. Though predictable, the pattern had grown to be an essential aspect of his existence.

Lily was sleeping in the tiny room next door, tucked up in the far corner of her bed, when he arrived. She was no longer the vivacious ball of enthusiasm that she once was. Instead, her eyes carried a quiet calm, a reflection of the changes that had seeped into their world over the past few years.

"Lily," Ash shook her shoulder. She stirred, blinking her eyes open. "Time to wake up."

Lily groggily rubbed her eyes, " Whiteout.. is Mom still in her room?"

Ash couldn't help but smile at the name. About a year ago, during one of their late-night drawing sessions, Lily had started calling him "Whiteout" after noticing how often he would stare blankly at a canvas, paralyzed by indecision and lost in thought. He'd laugh it off at first, but the name stuck. What began as a teasing jab became her term of endearment—a nod to his dreamy, scattered nature and untapped potential.

Yet, a knot tightened in his stomach. Ash hesitated to answer but said it anyway, as there wasn't an easy way to answer her question. "Yeah," he kept his voice steady as he said, "Go get ready. We need to leave for school."

Lily nodded and started getting ready for the day. Ash also didn't linger. He simply turned and headed downstairs. Although this wasn't a life they had imagined at such a young age, they had both learned not to ask too many questions. One day at a time, the patterns they followed all remained of a world that had been gradually vanishing from them.

Walking into the kitchen, Ash went through the motions of pulling out bread, peanut butter, jelly, and a small bag of apples, his hands working on autopilot while his mind drifted into the familiar recesses of his thoughts.

At just eleven years old, Ash had watched his world unravel. He could still remember the day everything began to shift. His father, once a steady and dependable presence, had buried himself so deeply in his work that he might as well have been a ghost in their home. Night after night, Ash and Lily would eat dinner with an empty chair at the head of the table, his dad's absence turning from occasional to constant. On the rare occasions his father did come home, it felt more like a fleeting visit than a return to family life—a miracle that left more questions than comfort.

And his mom? She had been the heart of the house once, always humming a tune, her hands guiding him and Lily at the piano or strumming her guitar with a joy that lit up the room. But that light had dimmed, replaced by a hollow version of the woman he used to know. The school where she had poured her passion into teaching music had let her go abruptly and without reasonable cause.

Ash still remembered overhearing the conversation between his parents late one night. His dad's clipped tone. His mom's quiet sobs. *Parents complained,* his father had said. *The kids weren't winning competitions under your mother's tutelage.* That was the day his mom's spark extinguished. Now she spent her days in her room, the once vibrant melodies she used to fill the house with replaced by silence.

Slathering peanut butter onto two slices of bread and following with jelly, Ash carefully assembled sandwiches for himself and Lily. He placed each into separate lunch bags, adding an apple to each one. He grabbed the last two granola bars from the cupboard, sliding them into the bags before sealing them.

Then, he poured cereal into two bowls, adding milk carefully so it wouldn't splash onto the counter. As he set the bowls on the small kitchen table, he called out, "Lily, breakfast is ready!"

He glanced at the eggs sitting on the counter, sighing. He'd wanted to make an omelet this morning, but his last few attempts had ended with burnt eggs and smoke filling the kitchen. Cereal would have to do for now, at least until he could learn how to cook properly without ruining everything.

Lily came into the kitchen, her backpack slung over one shoulder. She plopped into the chair and immediately began spooning cereal into her mouth with enthusiasm. Between bites, she muttered, "Milk and cereal again?"

Ash shrugged, sitting down across from her. "Just eat for now," his tone was even as he said, "I'll try to get better at making eggs so we can have more options."

Lily didn't argue; she just nodded and uttered, "Okay," before returning her attention to the bowl in front of her, humming softly between bites.

They ate in relative silence, the kind that had become normal between them—comfortable but tinged with the unspoken weight they both carried. Ash finished first, washing his bowl in the sink before heading back to his room. He reached into the top drawer of his desk, where a bottle of pills rested. Unscrewing the cap, he took out one of the small tablets and swallowed it with water.

ADHD was a word he had become all too familiar with, and he had decided to call it "The Static" to better reflect how he felt. After everything that had happened, his mind had struggled to keep up. The Siege, as he called the anxiety attacks, had become frequent and exhausting, leaving him feeling as if he were a balloon stretched too thin. Then, there was the Fog, a thick, unyielding haze of depression that dulled everything around him and made every step forward feel like a monumental effort.

It wasn't until Miss Thompson, his fifth-grade teacher at the time, took him to the hospital during one particularly bad episode that he finally got an explanation—ADHD mixed in with anxiety and depression. The diagnosis had been a relief in some ways, names for the storm raging in his head, but it also added to the list of things he felt his parents were trying and failing to manage in order to "fix" him into some normal version of what he should be.

They had tried at first. His mom would sit with him during his homework, gently reminding him to stay focused, while his dad would occasionally offer words of encouragement. But over time, as the cracks in their own lives widened, their support dwindled. Ash noticed it in the small things—his mom's tired sighs when he needed help, his dad's irritated tone when Ash forgot something important.

And then there was the essence.

Ash had come to call the pulsating colors that surrounded people as "essence." His father's once valiant gold aura had, over time, darkened into a murky brown. Ash could see the shift whenever his father looked at him, a mixture of guilt and frustration that lingered in the air. But it was the smoky haze he called "the grey" riding along the fringes of his father's essence, making the color even murkier. It stung more than the words his dad never said aloud: *I wish I could fix you.*

His mom's yellow had been completely taken over by the same "grey." The brightness was replaced by exhaustion and a brittle sadness that she no longer tried to hide behind a smile. The grey swirled around her, darkening her aura in moments of isolation, only to briefly flicker with small bursts of her original yellow when she had mustered enough energy to leave her room and do some work around the house.

Ash just couldn't understand her; one moment, she was distant, and the next, she would suddenly ask how Ash and Lily's day was. It was when he had heard his dad talking on the phone, referring to his Mom's sudden change as a result of being "bipolar." He hadn't understood the words at the time, but as Ash did his own research at school, Ash gradually came to understand that his Mom was suffering from "mood swings." He didn't know what they were, but just remembering his once sweet Mom turn into this unexpected ball of highs and lows made his heartache.

The most painful, though, was Lily's pink. She had always been his bright spot, her essence a vibrant pink that glowed with happiness at the smallest of things but had now become stained with worry and burden.

A deep blue bled into the edges, and the brightness rarely returned, not even when she sang. Ash used to watch her perform with awe, her aura lighting up like a firework. Now, when she sang, the spark never came back.

Ash felt the weight of their essence like a second skin, their emotions pressing in on him from all sides. He hated the guilt that curled in his stomach when he saw their colors darken, knowing he was part of the reason why. But even more, he hated how powerless he felt to fix it. Even if it wasn't really his fault, he felt responsible for helping alleviate the imposing grey and return them to a solid state.

Ash stepped into the hallway and moved toward his mother's room. Lily was already there, standing quietly in front of the door. "Mom," Ash called out gently, with a practiced calm that didn't betray the worry swirling inside him. "We're going to school now. Please take care of yourself, okay?"

Lily echoed him but with an edge of vulnerability. They waited for a response, but none came. The silence stretched, growing heavier with each second. Ash glanced at Lily, who kept her eyes fixed on the door, her jaw tightening slightly. After a long moment, Ash gave a small nod, signaling it was time to leave. Together, they turned and made their way out of the house.

The chill of the morning air greeted them as they stepped onto the street. Ash walked a step behind Lily, watching her blue aura shift as they approached the bus stop. The bus ride was quiet, the kind of stillness shared by sleepy teenagers lost in their own worlds. Ash and Lily sat side by side, their usual unspoken rhythm keeping them in sync. Ash glanced out the window, letting the blur of the city wash over him while Lily absentmindedly hummed under her breath.

The medication seemed to be doing its job. Ash could feel the familiar fog in his mind lifting, the sharp clarity that came when the Static medication began to take effect. Not only was his focus improving, but the overwhelming presence of the auras began to retreat, not completely, but enough to stop the constant pressure on his senses. It wasn't perfect, but it was a relief.

The edges of the colors became less jagged, and he didn't feel the familiar headache starting to form. His ears, too, weren't ringing with the intensity of everyone's emotions; they felt muted as if his senses were wrapped in a soft, cottony barrier.

But Ash knew it wouldn't last. As they arrived at school, Ash gave Lily a quick, warm smile, which she returned with a wide grin. She reached up to give him a brief hug, her arms wrapping around him in a gesture of reassurance, "See you, Whiteout." She pulled away and ran off toward her group of friends.

"Goodbye," Ash muttered, watching her go before turning to face the school building. A small, faint smile lingered on his lips for a moment, but it quickly faded.

Although the medication dulled the colors and noise, the chaotic energy of the school entrance still overwhelmed Ash. Bright reds of excitement, jagged yellows of chatter, and restless greens pulsed around him like strobe lights.

He sighed heavily, tugging his hoodie over his head as if the soft fabric could shield him from the sensory onslaught. Keeping his eyes fixed on the floor, he navigated the sea of bodies, weaving through the chaos with practiced precision.

The hallway offered little relief. The noise was sharper here, bouncing off the walls and mixing with the swirl of emotions bleeding into the air. Ash moved toward his locker, his hands trembling slightly as he reached for the lock. He twisted the combination quickly; his only thought was to get his things and escape to class before the sensory overload grew unbearable.

But then he felt it—a shift in the atmosphere.

The hairs on the back of his neck prickled as an unmistakable wave of hostility rolled toward him. The auras surrounding him darkened, their tones sharpening into aggressive reds tinged with muddy blacks. Ash turned slowly, his chest tightening as he met the cold and calculating gaze of Jackson Chen.

Jackson stood at the head of a small group of students, his thin frame draped in the latest fashion—an all-black hoodie and distressed jeans that seemed tailored to fit perfectly. His stringy black hair hung in uneven strands, partially covering his cold, dark eyes that glinted with calculated malice. The group behind him emanated the same volatile essence. Ash knew the collective group of regression as Raze, a clique notorious for their intimidating presence and penchant for picking on easy targets. They were the storm clouds that loomed over the school, and Ash had just been caught in their path.

"Hey, freak," Jackson called with mockery. The corners of his mouth curled into a cruel smirk as his friends chuckled behind him. Their essence pulsed in sync, a collective force of malice that crashed into Ash like a tidal wave.

Ash froze as the colors around them brightened to an almost unbearable intensity. His eyesight became blurry at the edges, and his chest constricted even more. The corridor seemed to be closing in on him, and the only sound he could hear was his own heartbeat.

"Got nothing to say?" Jackson took a step closer, his aura spiking with dominance. The others flanked him, their laughter echoing in Ash's ears like a taunt he couldn't escape.

Ash's breath came in shallow gasps as the anxiety gripped him fully. It was too much—the hues, the cacophony, the crushing weight of their aggressive desires. His trembling hands gripped his backpack's straps as though they could hold him in place as he leaned his back against the locker.

Entangled in a web of anxiety and self-doubt, his mind whirled. His rising panic seemed to cause the auras to become even brighter in reaction.

"Hey, Jackson!" The sharp voice cut through the haze of fear enveloping Ash, like sunlight piercing through storm clouds. He blinked, his eyes focusing on the figure now standing firmly between him and Jackson's group.

It was Lily.

Her blue aura, glowing with a calm intensity, immediately began to soothe Ash's frayed nerves. She crossed her arms, her sharp gaze fixed on Jackson. "What's your problem?" she demanded, making the laughter of Jackson's friends falter.

Jackson rolled his eyes, his bravado cracking under Lily's unflinching stare. "What? Ash needs his little sister to save him," he muttered.

"No more than you need yours to pass math class." Lily shot back, cold and unwavering. She took a step forward, subtly forcing Jackson and his crew to step back. Her aura pulsed bright like the time when it had been pink.

"Whatever," Jackson grumbled, turning to his friends. "Let's go." The group retreated, their auras dimming as they disappeared into the crowd.

Lily turned to Ash. Her blue aura enveloped him fully, pushing away the remnants of the tension. "Whiteout, are you okay?" she asked gently.

Ash nodded shakily, his breathing evening out as the oppressive aura of the group drifted away. "Thanks," he murmured.

Lily gave him a small smile, brushing an invisible speck off his hoodie, "You've got to stand up for yourself more. But don't worry. I still got your back." she said warmly. "Besides, Jackson knows I can cut him down to size because his sister and I are friends. He can't pass any of his classes without her." She chuckled internally, aware of Jackson's false bravado with others, but when it came to his sister, she could easily make his life more difficult, so he was far more cautious around her than anyone else.

Ash had always known his sister had an almost uncanny ability to sense when he was overwhelmed. She could spot the signs long before anyone else—his hunched shoulders, the way he avoided eye contact or the tremor in his hands. Without fail, she would step in, creating a buffer between him and the world when it became too much with the strength and intimidation of a full-grown adult.

This time was no different. Despite being a child herself, her essence acted as a shield, its calm waves quieting the storm in his mind.

"You want me to walk you to class?" Lily asked, tilting her head.

Ash shook his head, lips quirking into a faint smile. "No, I'm good," he said. "Thanks again."

Lily gave him a playful nudge. "Alright, but don't let them get to you, okay?" She turned and walked off, leaving behind a lingering sense of peace.

Ash watched her go, his shoulders relaxing. He adjusted his backpack and headed to class, the memory of her unwavering support bolstering him against the day ahead.

Ash walked into history class, the familiar creak of the door hinges announcing his arrival. Rows of desks filled quickly, the chatter of his classmates buzzing like a swarm of bees. He slid into his usual seat near the back, closest to the window, where he could steal glances at the trees swaying outside—a small escape when the pressure got too much.

Mr. Peterson, a stout man with a salt-and-pepper beard, stood at the front of the room, scribbling dates on the board. His aura was a muted blue, a sign of his usual calm demeanor. Ash breathed a little easier seeing it, but that relief was short-lived.

"Alright, everyone," Mr. Peterson began, turning to face the class with a folder in hand. "Clear your desks. We're going to have a quiz today."

A ripple of groans spread across the room, followed by the screech of chair legs against the linoleum as students begrudgingly complied. Ash froze. The word "quiz" reverberated in his mind like a warning siren, and suddenly the room felt stifling.

As the first few papers were passed down the rows, the energy in the room shifted. Auras around him flared erratically, buzzing in Ash's mind like an electric current, making his skin prickle and his pulse quicken.

The siege jolted directly to the forefront. The shifting colors distracted him, each aura screaming a different emotion. The scrape of a pencil against paper felt like nails on a chalkboard, and the ticking clock above the door amplified in his ears. He tried to focus on the quiz in front of him, but the words on the page blurred and danced, refusing to stay still.

Question One: *What year did the Treaty of Versailles come into effect?*

Ash closed his eyes for a moment, trying to summon the answer from memory. Instead, the chaotic waves of emotion in the room crashed into him like a storm. He tightened his grip on the pencil, willing himself to push through.

Breathe. Just breathe.

Ash dropped his pencil and squeezed his eyes shut. The darkness was soothing, even if only for a moment. With his vision gone, the overwhelming colors dulled, giving him a reprieve.

Reset. Focus.

He inhaled deeply and opened his eyes, forcing himself to read the first question again. He closed his eyes after writing his answer, repeating the cycle for the next question.

Slowly, the noise around him faded, his focus narrowing to just the quiz in front of him.

By the time he reached the final question, sweat beaded at his temple, but he'd done it. Ash looked up, meeting Mr. Peterson's gaze briefly.

After a drab review of the quiz material, the bell rang, signaling the end of class, and Ash exhaled in relief. He'd survived the first class of the day, but more importantly, he'd discovered something new about himself. Closing his eyes and refocusing, even for a second, helped him regain control.

It wasn't perfect, but it was a start.

The next class was biology, and as Ash made his way to the lab, the faint relief from history class began to fade. His stomach churned at the memory of what Mr. Tanaka, the Science teacher, had said last time: *"We'll be forming groups for a long-term project. Collaboration is key!"*

Collaboration. The word alone was enough to send Ash into a quiet spiral of dread. He hated group projects. Too many personalities, too much unspoken tension, and a chaotic blend of colors and energies that left him drained and defeated.

He slid into a seat near the back, hoping to avoid attention, but Mr. Tanaka was already handing out group assignments. The teacher's aura was a bright yellow—enthusiastic and focused—which clashed with Ash's growing unease.

"Ash, you'll be with Laila, Connor, and Jasmine," Mr. Tanaka announced, pointing toward three other students scattered across the room.

Ash's heart sank as the four of them awkwardly gathered around a lab table. Ash could feel the tension rising immediately, their auras clashing like off-key instruments.

"So, uh, what's the project again?" Connor asked, tapping his pencil on the table rhythmically. His orange aura vibrated with an almost aggressive energy, pulling Ash's attention like a flashing neon sign.

"We're supposed to design an experiment related to plant growth," Jasmine said curtly, her green aura calm but cold.

"Should we... brainstorm ideas?" Laila offered timidly, her yellow aura flickering like a candle in a draft.

Ash tried to focus, but their overlapping emotions made it impossible. Each one pulled at him, demanding his attention. Connor's restless energy made Ash's skin crawl. Laila's nervousness tugged at his heart, while Jasmine's clinical detachment left him feeling excluded.

"Okay, so, like... what if we do something with music and plants?" Connor suggested, grinning as he mimed strumming a guitar.

"That's been done a million times," Jasmine snapped. "We need something original."

"Well, do *you* have a better idea?" Connor shot back.

Laila shrank back; her yellow essence flickered before flaring into a bright, blinding orange along with an ear-ringing barrage of sounds. The intense colors and sound sent a jolt through his body, making Ash squeeze his eyes shut and move away, pressing his hands against his ears. Even though his actions weren't subtle, no one paid him any heed.

Instead, the conversation devolved into bickering, their voices rising and overlapping. The emotional waves crashed over Ash, each one louder and more intense than the last. He wanted to close his eyes, to block out the chaos and reset, but there was no time. Every second he spent disengaged felt like another missed opportunity to contribute, another way he might let the group down.

"Uh, guys," Ash finally managed to say, barely audible over the noise. "Maybe we should—"

"Can't you just pick a side or something?" Connor interrupted, his gaze snapping to Ash. "We're wasting time."

Ash froze, the pressure of their expectations pressing down on him. He couldn't think, couldn't breathe. His hands trembled as he fumbled with his pencil.

"I—" He faltered, the words refusing to come.

Jasmine rolled her eyes, muttering something under her breath, while Laila offered an apologetic look. Connor sighed dramatically, throwing his hands up.

"Fine, whatever. Let's just vote or something," Connor said, clearly exasperated.

Ash stared down at the table, his mind spinning. He had no idea what they were even voting on. His chance to contribute had slipped through his fingers, leaving him feeling insignificant and invisible and most of all, disappointed in himself that he couldn't just speak out and say what he thought.

The rest of the meeting blurred together in a haze of stress and frustration. When the bell finally rang, Ash bolted from the room. In the hallway, he leaned against the cool metal of a locker, closing his eyes at last. The world felt quieter, calmer, but the after-taste of his failure lingered.

His new coping strategy had been no match for the chaos of group dynamics. He needed something more to help him navigate a world that never seemed to slow down.

When Ash finally made it home, his head throbbed with everything that had taken place. However, the day was far from over. Not only did he have home assignments and the group project to work on, but he also had to prepare a meal for himself, his sister Lily, and even his mom.

But when he and Lily walked into the kitchen, their expectations quickly shifted. On the counter was a small meal—nothing extravagant, just a few simple sandwiches, some fruit, and a warm bowl of soup. It was clear their mother had made it. It was a rare but precious occurrence when she was feeling better.

Ash and Lily shared a quiet, comforting meal together. It was simple, but there was a warmth to it that felt like a breath of fresh air amidst the storm of their lives. When they finished, the two of them walked quietly to their mother's room.

"Thank you for dinner, Mom," Ash's voice was full of gratitude that never quite found a way to express itself.

Lily echoed his sentiment.

Their mother didn't respond, but they didn't push her; they simply retreated back into their own rooms, giving her space. Ash went to his room, the hum of the house fading into the background as he sank onto his bed. There was nothing he could do about the pressure, but for now, there was a brief lull in the storm. He decided it was time to do something he had been meaning to do for a while.

Pulling out a worn notebook from beneath his bed, he opened it to a fresh page. The first thing he wrote was a title:

Observations of the Essence

Then he began to write:

"Today, I learned something new about myself. I've been thinking about how emotions from the people around me affect me and how I can't always filter them out. In history class, I felt the pressure of everyone's anxiety when Mr. Peterson announced the quiz. I felt as if I couldn't breathe. Their emotions were so overwhelming that I couldn't even focus on my own paper. That's when I learned the trick to close my eyes and reset. It didn't work perfectly, but it helped me get through the quiz.

In biology, things were worse. The project meeting... too many emotions at once. Laila's yellow, Connor's orange, Jasmine's green—they were all pulling on me. I couldn't stop it. I couldn't find a way to focus or contribute because the emotions were too loud. I felt like I was drowning in them. I didn't have the time to close my eyes or take a breather. I was overwhelmed before it even started."

Ash paused and looked down at the page. He wasn't sure if he could ever fully explain what it felt like, but this was a start. He continued:

"I've been wondering if I could make sense of the way these emotions work, the way people's auras clash or align. Maybe I could learn how to read them and control them. Maybe it could help me deal with school, with The Static, with everything."

He flipped the page and added a few more thoughts about his day, about his group project, about the constant battle of trying to focus and filter the world around him. His observations were becoming more detailed and more precise. He had never written anything like this before, but it felt important. It felt like the first real step toward understanding his gift instead of just surviving it.

As he wrote, Ash realized his words were falling short, unable to fully convey what he was experiencing. He couldn't describe the constant shifting of colors, the intensity of emotions blending together. So, without thinking much about it, he began to draw.

The first sketch was a blur of yellow, orange, and green, trying to capture the essence of Laila, Connor, and Jasmine as their emotions mingled and pulsed around them. He drew the subtle shifts—Laila's yellow dimming into an anxious, flickering orange, Connor's orange darkening into a deep, almost dangerous red. With each new sketch, he tried to map out how their colors twisted and blended, the way emotional pressure made their essences shift. He realized that the color wasn't just a random change—it had meaning. As they were pushed to their limits, their colors grew darker and more muddled, as if losing themselves in the emotional chaos. The change wasn't just temporary—it seemed to build up over time, slowly becoming permanent as people's emotional states evolved.

Drawing these patterns, Ash saw something undeniable: the color shifts were tied to emotional development, growth, or deterioration. When a person was under pressure, their colors blended with the emotions around them, and eventually, those colors became so dark and unrecognizable that they almost lost their essence altogether.

With a deep breath, he closed the notebook and slid it beneath the loose floorboard in his room. It felt symbolic, hiding the thoughts away for now, knowing that they were just the beginning of something larger. He didn't know how he would figure this all out, but this journal was his first real attempt at taking control.

Chapter 4: The Language of Colors

The morning light filtered through the curtains, casting a soft glow across Ash's room as he slowly woke. Yesterday's chaotic memories still pressed on him, but today felt different. It was a new day, a chance to make things better. He resolved silently to let it pass with more control, to allow himself to breathe without getting lost in the overwhelming emotional waves that seemed to follow him wherever he went.

He slipped into his black oversized hoodie, the fabric enveloping him like a shield. The hood came up to cover his head, just enough for him to avoid meeting anyone's eyes or seeing their essence.

After washing up and brushing his teeth, Ash packed a pair of sunglasses and headphones into his bag. He wasn't sure if it would work, but he had an idea. Maybe, just maybe, the sunglasses could help him shield his eyes from the bright, flashing auras of those around him. He knew they wouldn't be allowed in class, but he figured if he could at least get to the classroom without being overwhelmed, it would be progress. The headphones were his backup, meant to dull the overwhelming sounds that always seemed to follow the essence. Ash was hopeful, even if only for a brief moment, that today would go better.

He popped one of his "Static" medications and walked over to his sister's room. "Lily, wake up and go get fresh," he called loud enough to rouse her from sleep.

As she shuffled off to get ready, Ash moved to the kitchen. The thought of peanut butter and jelly sandwiches every day had started to wear on him. They couldn't keep eating the same thing all the time—there had to be a way to get more nutrients without complicating things too much. He decided to try boiled eggs, something simple but nutritious.

He carefully placed four eggs in a pot, filled it with water, and set the heat on low, covering it with a lid. Although he felt his pulse quicken, afraid of getting burned, he forced himself to stay calm.

As the eggs boiled, he got to work preparing the rest of their breakfast and lunch. With steady hands, he carefully sliced the tomatoes, focusing on avoiding any accidental nicks from the knife. The tomatoes were placed into a hot oiled pan with a pinch of salt, and the sizzling sound filled the room.

When the tomatoes were fried and set aside, Ash placed the bread in the pan, adding cheese on top and then the warm, tender tomatoes. He pressed them together, making a grilled cheese sandwich with a twist. Just as the sandwich finished cooking, he checked on the eggs. He felt the heat radiating off the pot as he carefully lifted each egg with a spoon, wincing as the pan's surface seemed to burn into his hands.

His patience was tested as he attempted to crack the eggs open immediately, but the outer shell burned his fingers. "Ow!" he yelped, unable to suppress the cry of pain.

Hearing him, Lily came rushing down the stairs. "What happened?" she asked.

Ash shook his hands lightly, trying to dull the pain as he said, "Nothing. I was just being an idiot and grabbed the eggs while they were hot."

Lily's calm blue aura flickered in understanding, and she stepped forward. "Here, give it to me. I know how to do it."

Ash hesitated, surprised. "You do?"

Lily smiled, nodding. "Yeah, my friend's mom does it like this."

With delicate care, Lily took the eggs from him, her fingers working slowly as Ash watched with anxiety. "Be careful, it's hot," he warned, but Lily was unfazed. She cracked the first egg with precision, and it opened perfectly.

She smiled at the result, her calm blue aura flickering with satisfaction. Ash let out a breath he hadn't realized he was holding as she cracked the second egg. His hands were still shaking, but the pressure lifted slightly with each successful crack.

When all four eggs were cracked open, Ash couldn't help but let out a relieved sigh. But his moment of relief was short-lived. As he sliced the egg into two halves, his smile faded. The middle of the egg didn't seem right. He stared at the yolk, which seemed slightly undercooked, a small but noticeable flaw.

"Did it not cook well?" Ash whispered with disappointment.

Lily didn't hesitate; she bit into one half of the egg and then shook her head, smiling gently. "Nope, it's perfect, Whiteout." Ash stared at her, waiting for any sign of hesitation, but she continued eating, her face lighting up with approval.

When she said nothing but continued eating with a smile, Ash's heart softened, the tension slowly melting away in that small, shared moment of joy.

They quickly finished their breakfast, gathering their things as the clock ticked closer to the time they needed to leave. Ash wrapped the plate with a boiled egg and grilled cheese sandwich in a glass cover, making sure it was secure before heading toward their mother's room. He knocked softly on the door.

"Mom, we'll be going now. I'm leaving some breakfast out here for you. If you're hungry, please have it," Ash said as loudly as he could so it would reach his Mom across the door.

Without waiting for a response, both Ash and Lily hurried out of the house. The urgency of getting to school spurred them forward.

Just as the front door closed behind them, their mother's room opened with a click.

***

Stepping out the door, Ash fished out his sunglasses and headphones. He adjusted the headphones on his ears and the sunglasses on his eyes. The combination of both items sitting together on his face was awkward, but Ash forced it, pulling the hood of his black oversized hoodie up to shield himself further.

Lily glanced over at him with a hint of curiosity but didn't ask any questions—she knew better. Instead, she gave him a small nod and turned toward the bus stop. Ash followed her silently, hoping that this would work.

When they reached the bus, Lily boarded first, taking her usual seat. Ash made his way to the back, trying to keep to himself as much as possible. The extra items on him proved effective, maybe not 100%, but they helped.

The kids around him shifted away, whispering and casting sidelong glances at his appearance. Their voices buzzed like background static, but Ash barely noticed. He let the moments slide by, his focus steady, the hum of lo-fi beats pouring into his ears. The soft, ambient rhythm flowed through his thoughts, each mellow chord unraveling the knots in his mind.

Behind the tinted glass of his sunglasses, the kaleidoscope of others' vibrant auras dulled. Swirling blues and oranges blurred into muted tones—distant, unimportant. His heart slowed, the tension in his chest easing as calm settled over him.

Lo-fi always did this—steady and uncomplicated, a soundtrack smoothing the jagged edges of his mind. It wasn't his favorite, though. His favorite songs lived in the past, soundtracking easier days when happiness came effortlessly.

Back then, his parents blasted oldies from the '80s and '90s. Those songs carried the memory of sun-filled Saturdays, long car rides with the windows down, and kitchen dance sessions full of laughter. Fleetwood Mac, Boyz II Men, Prince—each note a piece of a simpler, brighter world. He could still hear his mother's off-key singing, her sunshine-yellow aura radiant with joy.

The nostalgia tugged at his heart, but he let it drift away. Today wasn't for memories. The lo-fi rhythm kept him grounded. He wasn't running from anything. For now, he was content to just *be*—rooted in the moment, with the beats anchoring his breath.

When they reached their stop, the bus doors opened, and Lily gave him a quick glance before slipping off the bus with the usual ease. Ash followed; his footsteps paced. As they neared the school, Lily casually greeted, "Goodbye, Whiteout. I'll catch you later."

Ash waved with a small smile, staying where he was for a moment longer, watching Lily go, before he turned and headed to his destination.

His stomach tightened as he walked. Yesterday's incident with Jackson still lingered in the back of his mind. He didn't want to face him again, not today. Ash quickened his pace, his heart beating faster as he neared the lockers.

When he reached his locker, he shoved the combination in, grabbed what he needed for his first class, and slammed the door shut with a little too much force. He didn't bother to look around, just hurried down the hall, making sure to avoid any lingering crowds. The last thing he needed was to run into Jackson or his crew.

To Ash's relief, as he made his way into the classroom, Jackson and his small group of "hounds" weren't around. For once, it seemed like the universe was cutting him a break.

***

The day dragged on until lunchtime finally came around. Ash started heading toward the library to meet his groupmates for the dreaded project. Connor was already there, tapping his fingers impatiently on the table. Laila and Jasmine were chatting quietly, their moods set in a tense air.

"Finally, everyone's here," Connor glanced up when Ash arrived. "Can we get started now? I want to finish this fast so I can have my lunch."

Jasmine shot him a look that could freeze water. "We'll stay as long as we need to, Connor. It's not only your group project, and I want a good grade."

Laila, clearly uncomfortable with the escalating tension, tried to pitch in. "Well, how about we do it after school? We can go to someone's house and work then."

But both Jasmine and Connor snapped at her almost in unison. "We're already here, Laila," Jasmine muttered.

Ash could feel the tension building. The words, the harsh tones, and the clash of ideas all stirred a violent mix of colors and noises. He closed his eyes, hoping to block it all out, to breathe through the chaos.

As his mind struggled to stay focused, the world became a swirl of bright, harsh colors. He felt himself slipping, but slowly, the storm seemed to quiet just enough for him to pull out the small sketchbook his father had bought him years ago. The pages felt familiar, grounding him in some small way. Ash grabbed his colors and began sketching, drawing random shapes and colors to find a semblance of peace.

As he worked, the bickering around him began to quiet down. The sharp words faded into the background as Ash's focus narrowed to the soft strokes of his colors on paper. He wasn't sure how long it had been, but when he finally looked up, the group had gone silent. All three of his groupmates were staring at him.

"What are you doing?" Connor asked with curiosity.

Ash hesitated for a moment before responding, "I'm drawing. It helps me think.."

Connor leaned in, pushing his head close to Ash's notebook, "What are you drawing?" His eyes were wide, inspecting the colors Ash had used. "Hmm... Wow, is that orange or red? It looks like lava," he mused.

Ash nodded slightly, unsure what to make of Connor's sudden interest.

Connor's eyes lit up. "Hey, I've got an idea," he said, almost excited. "I mean, it's a common experiment, but how about we make an active volcano model? It would be pretty cool, right?"

Jasmine thought for a moment, her interest piqued, "I guess that's interesting, but it's kind of common. Is there any way we can make it unique somehow?"

Laila hesitated, her aura flickering in a mix of yellow and orange as she bit her lip. Ash watched her, noticing the subtle shift in her energy. "Laila, do you have an idea?" he asked.

At first, Laila seemed taken aback, surprised by the attention. But as the group's eyes turned to her, she took a deep breath and spoke in a rush. "Yes, um… what if we added trees, a river, and built a whole forest around the volcano? We could show that the volcano has already erupted and how it affected the surrounding area, like the local people and their homes."

She let out the rest of her sentence in one go, not pausing for air. For a moment, no one spoke. Ash's heart pounded in his chest. His eyes flicked from one person to the next, waiting for a reaction.

Connor was the first to respond, smiling, "That's a great idea, Laila!"

Jasmine nodded in agreement, "Yeah, that could work. Now, all we need is to figure out the distribution of tasks."

The rest of the meeting went smoothly after that. Ash was assigned the task of painting the volcano and landscaping—something he was more than happy to do, given his natural talent for drawing and coloring.

Things were going well, better than ever. He was even happier that he hadn't had to step foot in the cafeteria. That place was a sensory nightmare, a cauldron of emotions, violent colors clashing in every corner, and deafening noise that made his head throb. Instead, he ate his lunch at the table, sharing some of it with Connor.

Connor had raised a brow when Ash offered half of his grilled cheese and boiled egg. "You made this?" he asked, incredulous. "Man, I can barely boil water."

Ash only shrugged, feeling a small flicker of pride as he bit into his sandwich. The good mood stayed with him most of the day. He allowed himself to settle into the flow of classes and let the hours pass without tension. But reality had a way of crashing in when he least expected it.

In the last class of the day, everything shifted again.

He was sitting quietly, head down, focusing on the lines of his notebook when the teacher's sharp voice cut through the classroom.

"Ash?"

He blinked and looked up.

"Why do you have your hoodie up?"

Ash hesitated. His heart began to race. "I—"

"This isn't a fashion show," the teacher snapped. "Pull it down so I can see your face. Now. Or you'll have to leave my class."

His fists clenched, nails digging into his palms. A tremor worked its way up his arms as he slowly pulled the hoodie down. His hair simply puffed up like a baby chick.

The snickers started immediately.

"Nice hair, Ash!"

Ash ignored the words, but they weren't what hurt the most. No, it was the violent bursts of color radiating from their auras—sharp reds, mocking greens, bitter browns—all crashing together in a cacophony of sound and chaos. The noise of it was unbearable, like a roaring ocean of static in his ears. The letters on the page in front of him blurred into meaningless streaks of black.

The teacher tapped her desk with a ruler. "Now. Go ahead and read the passage, Ash."

Ash's throat tightened. His mouth opened, but nothing came out. His mind swam, drowning in the overwhelming hues and clashing sounds.

"Can't even read? Figures," someone muttered.

"Stay quiet, all of you."

The voice rang out clear and strong, cutting through the noise like sunlight piercing a storm. Ash felt the chaos recede like a tide pulling away from shore. He looked up.

There, near the center of the room, sat Addie Madison, half-turned in her seat. Her vibrant emerald essence stood out like a beacon of calm amidst the swirling mess of colors. It didn't hurt his eyes. It didn't make his ears ring. Her presence was like the scent of a forest after rain, fresh and pure.

Addie Madison was the most popular girl who had charmed the teachers and students alike. She had led her basketball team to victory and could win a fight against the guys if she had to. Addie was fierce and free, like the wild heart of nature itself. Her essence undermined everyone else's, not even a speck of dust dimming her shine.

She turned her bright eyes to him and smiled gently. "Go ahead, Ash. Read."

The calm in her voice worked its way into his chest, soothing the storm raging inside. The words in front of him slowly came into focus. He drew a breath, steadied his hand, and began to read.

***

As they walked home that afternoon, Ash felt a lightness in his step that he hadn't experienced in a long time. The headphones dangled around his neck, and his sunglasses sat in his pocket. The colors that had always tangled around him had faded into soft, manageable hues. His sister, Lily, couldn't help but notice. She tilted her head, her eyes bright with curiosity.

"Ash," she asked, "you seem different today… did something good happen?"

Ash glanced at her, the faintest trace of a smile tugging at his lips. But he only shook his head and kept walking. It wasn't that he didn't want to share it with Lily; it was just that he felt if he spoke it out, the good feeling would disappear faster.

When they stepped into the house, Ash removed his sunglasses and headphones, holding them carefully in his hands. He didn't tuck them away in his bag. He couldn't risk his safety nets being crushed or broken. Then he noticed that the air in the house was different. As they entered the kitchen, they both stopped short.

Their mother was there.

She stood near the counter, her thin frame silhouetted against the late afternoon light. A steaming cup of coffee rested in her hands, the rich aroma swirling softly around her. Her dark hair fell limply over her shoulders, and though her expression was unusually serene, a faint flicker of something lighter played at the corners of her lips.

She didn't come out of her room often, but when she did, it added a lightness to the air, a subtle shift in the weight of the house. Her presence, rare as it was, reminded Ash of things that had been set aside but not entirely forgotten. The closed door was becoming too much a part of the house, like the walls and windows—something to pass without notice. But seeing her now, coffee in hand and her eyes on the open book lying beside her, it was almost pleasant—almost like how it used to be.

"Mom?" Lily's voice was a mix of hope and hesitation. "Are you feeling okay?"

Their mother turned, a smile flickering across her lips. For a moment, Ash saw a glimmer of yellow in her essence—a faint, fleeting trace of the brightness she used to have. Her tired eyes lingered on Ash and Lily as they entered the room. She smiled faintly, but there was a hollow quality to it like she was struggling to find the energy to keep it up.

"So, how was school today?" she asked, though her mind seemed far away.

Lily eagerly began telling her about the lunch they'd had, excited to share that Ash had made something special. "It was really cool, Mom. Ash made these awesome sandwiches, and we tried these new chips—"

But her mother interrupted before Lily could finish, her face falling. "I'm sorry I didn't make you anything today. I should've. I should be doing more for you two. You deserve a better mom than this..." She trailed off, her countenance thick with guilt.

Ash felt the tension growing, the familiar heaviness settling in the room. He looked at Lily, unsure of what to say. Lily, trying to help, gently spoke up.

"Mom, we know you're doing the best you can right now," she said, trying to ease the burden she could see her mother carrying. "Ash was just trying something different for lunch. It's not a big deal."

But her mother's eyes darkened, the smoke completely taking over, "I think I am still too tired. I should go back to my room now."

Slowly, she turned and disappeared into the house. The door to her room closed with a soft click, and as it did, Ash saw the black haze follow her.

For a moment, neither Ash nor Lily moved. The air felt heavier again, thick with unspoken things. It was Lily who finally broke the silence.

"Are you okay?" she asked gently.

Ash nodded, though his limbs felt shaky, "I'm good. I… I think I'll make dinner after I rest a bit. Okay?"

Lily placed a hand on his shoulder. "Don't worry about it, Ash."

He shook his head, his resolve firm. "We have to eat, Lily. Someone has to cook."

She frowned, realizing what he meant. There wasn't anything on the counter except for an empty plate in the drying rack—washed, dried, and put aside.

Ash swallowed hard. It was the plate he had set out with breakfast that morning. His mother had eaten it. That alone was enough to kindle a faint spark of warmth in his chest.

She had eaten. She had tried.

And that was enough for now.

***

The soft hum of the library's fluorescent lights was a dull backdrop as Ash sat hunched over his project, the paints and brushes scattered around him. He dragged a brush across the figurine, but his mind replayed yesterday's events—his mother's sudden shift in mood when Lily mentioned the lunch he made.

Her face had changed so quickly, her essence darkening. The air thickened with her guilt, and the gray settled in. Her apology for not doing more for them lingered in his mind, and now, as his brush stroked the figurine, he realized how his actions had pulled her deeper into that darkness.

His hand slipped, breaking the figurine. He stared at the broken piece, his breath catching painfully. His mother's words echoed in his mind, tightening the knot of anxiety in his chest.

His breath grew shallow, and the pressure inside him became unbearable. Ash set the figurine down, the broken pieces mirroring his own fractured thoughts. Something heavy settled in his chest, like an anchor he couldn't untie.

Not here… not now.

His eyes darted around the room. He needed somewhere quiet, somewhere away from prying eyes. If he could just get to a corner, maybe he could settle himself. But his legs felt like lead as he pushed back from the table. The effort to stand was a mountain too steep. His knees buckled, and he pitched forward, landing with a thud against the cold, hard floor.

"Oh no! Hey, are you okay?"

The words came from somewhere above him, urgent and familiar. He felt a hand on his shoulder, gently shaking him. "Ash? Hey, Ash? Breathe, it's me… Addie."

His mind swirled with panic, but the warmth in her voice tugged at his consciousness, anchoring him just enough to focus. He felt her shift beside him, leaning close. "Okay, listen to me. I know this feels awful, but you're going to be okay. Just try to follow my lead."

He wanted to tell her he couldn't, that his lungs weren't working, that his heart was thundering too fast to catch. But he remained speechless.

"Look at me," she whispered. "I have something to show you."

He managed to lift his eyes. Her face hovered close, her brows knit with concern. "See this?" She crossed her eyes dramatically and stuck out her tongue.

Despite himself, a tiny flicker of amusement sparked in his chest.

"Yeah, you like that? I can do more. Watch this." She puckered her lips, blew a raspberry, then scrunched her nose as if she'd smelled something terrible. Her antics were so ridiculous, so over-the-top, that a laugh bubbled up in his throat.

"There we go!" Addie grinned, her eyes bright with relief. "Keep it coming, Ash. Deep breaths now. Count with me, okay? One…"

He took a shaky inhale, her steady gaze guiding him.

"Two…"

Another breath, deeper this time.

"Three. You're doing it."

The air flowed easier now, and his heartbeat slowed as he rested his forehead against his arm, exhausted but feeling considerably better.

They sat in silence for a moment. The world around them seemed far away, the library's hushed stillness wrapping them in a bubble of quiet safety.

"Thanks," he murmured hoarsely.

Addie waved a hand dismissively. "Anytime. I mean, I had to save you. Who else is going to appreciate my incredible skills?"

Ash let out a soft laugh, "Incredible… is a strong word."

"Hey, now!" She poked his shoulder playfully. "That's gratitude for you."

"I have panic attacks too sometimes, and I have found that focusing on something else while taking steady breaths, like you did just now, helps."

They shared a quiet smile, a moment of connection forming between them like a bridge.

"By the way, what are you doing here?" Addie asked, scanning the mess of paintbrushes, paints, and clay figurines strewn across the table. Her eyes fell on the broken tree, "Is that your project? That tree broke? Is that why you were panicking?"

Ash blinked, overwhelmed by her rapid-fire questions. He started to speak but stumbled over his words. "I... It just... Yeah, I guess... I mean, sort of."

Addie grinned, a spark of energy dancing in her eyes. "Hey, let's go!"

Ash tilted his head, confused. "What? Where?"

"Of course, you'd feel suffocated in the library," she said matter-of-factly, already gathering his materials. "Let's get out of here and do your work outside. It's a beautiful day. Come on, I'll help."

Before Ash could protest, she had scooped up his project material. He grabbed the rest of his things and then stumbled after her.

The courtyard was alive with the hum of conversation and laughter. Ash hesitated; he wasn't used to working outside or being surrounded by so many people. His hands fidgeted with the edge of his notebook, but in comparison to Addie's beautiful emerald essence, everything faded away. So he followed Addie to a quiet corner under a sprawling oak tree.

The sun filtered through its leaves, dappling the ground with golden light. She plopped onto the grass, spreading his supplies between them.

He sat down, too, his heart still beating faster than he liked. Oblivious to his unease, Addie held up the broken tree and started fixing it.

"We'll fix this," she said confidently.

As Ash watched her work, something inside him relaxed. There was something about her voice, the way her hands moved with certainty, as she laid out the contents of her own bag and started reattaching the two halves of the tree.

He picked up another tree figurine and started working on coloring it the dull green. Beside him, Addie talked about everything and nothing, her words a soothing background hum. She laughed as a breeze tugged at her hair, pushing it into her eyes. She made no attempt to fix it, and Ash found himself smiling.

"See? Fresh air and sunlight make a difference," she said, stretching her arms toward the sky. "I always come out here when I need to clear my head."

Ash's eyes drifted to her aura. It shifted with her mood— a vibrant morning green when she laughed, softening to a calmer evening jade as she fell silent and watched him work. She had no idea he could see it, no clue how her colors captivated him.

"You draw like you're carving something real," she said, watching his careful strokes. "Like you're bringing it to life."

He flushed. "It helps me think."

"Thinking's overrated," Addie quipped. Then, her voice grew softer. "Or maybe we just think too much about the wrong things."

He glanced at her sideways. "What do you mean?"

She leaned back, propping herself up on her hands. "I have this thing where I feel like I have to be perfect. All the time. My family…" she said, her eyes clouded, "They expect a lot. And sometimes, it feels like I can't mess up. Ever. Like if I do, everything falls apart."

Ash's chest tightened as he watched "the grey" seep deeper into her essence, darkening the brightness he had come to associate with her. It was the same shade that had slowly bled into his mother's radiant yellow, a subtle fog at first that grew thicker and heavier until it consumed her completely. His heart ached at the memory, the helplessness pressing against his ribs. He didn't want Addie to turn like that.

So he listened and tried to comfort her. "I get that. Except it's my brain that won't let me get things right. It's like there are too many thoughts at once, and they trip over each other. I can't catch my breath when it happens. It's… it's exhausting."

Their eyes met, understanding passing between them like a silent thread. Slowly, the haze seeped out of her emerald essence, and Ash heaved a sigh of relief.

Addie bumped her shoulder lightly against his. "Guess we're a good pair then. Your overthinking and my perfectionism might cancel each other out."

Ash chuckled, feeling lighter than he had all day. "Maybe."

They continued working side by side, a peaceful rhythm settling between them. She told stories and made him laugh, her presence a buffer against the world that usually felt too loud and too fast. He focused on his sketch, each careful line feeling more steady, more certain.

For the first time in a long while, Ash could enjoy the real world again.

Chapter 5: Family Reflections

The house was still, the air thick with the quiet hum of midnight. Ash was barely drifting in and out of sleep when he heard the unmistakable sound of the front door creaking open, slicing through the silence like a knife. His eyes shot open, heart racing.

"Who's there?" he wondered.

The house, usually peaceful, suddenly felt foreign. With his father away for weeks and his mother locked in her room, Ash's mind spiraled with unsettling possibilities. Lily slept soundly, blissfully unaware. He was the only one awake, the only one who could protect them, and the weight of that responsibility pressed heavily on his chest.

In a state of panic, Ash leaped out of bed, his heart pounding in his ears. Grabbing the broomstick from the corner of his room, he held it in trembling hands, clinging to it as if it could shield him from whatever lurked in the dark.

"I have to protect them," he thought.

He crept down the stairs, careful to avoid making a sound. The darkness seemed to close in around him, swallowing him whole, but he pushed forward. His breath was quick and shallow, his mind racing with thoughts that gripped his heart.

Just when he reached the bottom of the stairs, a faint murmur of voices drifted through the air. He froze, gripping the broomstick tighter, eyes widening as he realized the voice sounded familiar.

Could it be...?

He leaned around the corner, heart racing. There, standing in the entryway, was none other than his father. He hadn't been home in two weeks.

Ash blinked, still in shock. The copper streaks of his father's essence had meshed together into a murky brown under the dim light. His expression was weary and frustrated, his clothes a mess. As Ash continued to observe his father from a distance, his heart dropped at the sight of the bandages on his father's hand.

"Dad?" Ash's voice cracked, torn between calling out or retreating to his room.

His father stiffened, startled, their eyes locking for a moment. A flicker of surprise crossed his features as he noticed the broomstick in Ash's hands before focusing on his son.

"What are you doing awake at this hour, Ash?"

Despite his father's tired tone, there was an undercurrent of something else that Ash couldn't place.

Ash glanced down at the broomstick, suddenly feeling silly. "I thought a burglar had come in," he said.

His father studied him intently with narrowed eyes as though assessing something. Then he let out a tired sigh.

"Go back to sleep," he said almost dismissively. "Don't you have school tomorrow?"

Ash shook his head, the cold air brushing against his skin. "No. It's the weekend. School's off on weekends."

His father paused, Ash's words registering slowly.

Letting the broomstick lean against the wall, Ash studied his father's bandaged hand, realizing it explained the struggle his dad appeared to have at the entrance. He was trying to lift his bags but was limited by one hand.

"What happened to your hand, Dad?" Ash asked, concern slipping through the earlier tension.

His father looked at him for a long moment and averted his gaze before shrugging it off with a quick, dismissive reply. "Nothing. Just a little workplace accident."

Ash felt a knot tighten in his stomach. Although his father shrugged it off, a gray fracture rippled through his copper essence. It was anything but reassuring. Concerned, he stepped forward to take his father's bag.

"Let me help you," Ash said, trying to sound casual. As he picked it up, the weight nearly dragged him back down to Earth. He winced at the heaviness. "This is heavy! What's in here?"

His father hesitated. "Clothes to change into."

Ash nodded without saying anything. He knew his father had packed an insane amount of clothes when he last left for work; he just hadn't realized it would weigh this much. It was clear his father didn't want to come home. The awkward silence between them deepened as they walked through the house, the quiet stretching longer with each step. Ash felt an urge to fill the void, to say something—anything.

"Are you hungry, Dad?" Ash asked, hopeful. "If you want, I can make something. I've gotten pretty good at cooking, you know."

His father's eyes widened, and for a split second, Ash saw shock flicker across his face. "What do you mean you'll make something?" he asked, disbelief thick in his tone. "You're still a child."

Ash shrugged, a slight smile on his face. "So? It's not that difficult. I can make a really good omelet now if you want."

His father blinked, taken aback by Ash's response. But before he could reply, he shook his head, letting the moment slip away. "No, it's fine. I ate earlier. Now, let's go back to sleep."

Ash nodded, accompanying his father to his room. Just before his father stepped inside, Ash spoke again, quieter this time, hope lacing his voice.

"Dad?"

His father paused, turning back, his expression worn out. "Yes?"

"Does this mean you'll be home tomorrow too?" Ash asked, eagerness clear in his tone.

His father hesitated for a moment before answering. "Yeah. I'll be working from home for a few days."

Ash smiled, warmth spreading between them. "That's awesome."

Turning to leave, he returned to his room. The quiet of the house felt different now, less eerie with his father back. He settled into his bed, the blankets bringing a sense of comfort. With his father's presence, Ash felt a flicker of relief wash over him.

His eyes grew heavy, and soon, the events of the night faded away as he fell into a deep, uninterrupted sleep.

***

The next morning, Ash awoke to indistinct sounds coming up from downstairs. Still groggy from sleep, he rubbed his eyes, wondering what was going on. The house, which had felt peaceful and quiet just hours before, now carried an air of tension.

He paused for a moment, listening, then heard voices— low and sharp—rising from the kitchen. Ash furrowed his brow. He threw off his blanket and quietly padded down the hallway, trying not to make a sound.

As he reached the stairs, he spotted Lily peeking around the corner. Her wide eyes met his, and she pressed a finger to her lips, motioning for him to be quiet. Ash, puzzled, stepped forward cautiously, joining her at the threshold.

"What's going on?" he whispered.

Lily didn't respond immediately but gestured toward the kitchen, a nervous flicker in her eyes. Ash's curiosity piqued as he leaned slightly forward to peek around the corner.

What he saw made his stomach sink.

His parents were in the kitchen, standing too close for comfort. His father's posture was rigid, his jaw tight as he spoke in a low, angry voice. "How have you been handling things?"

His mother shot back with a bitter retort. "At least I didn't leave home like a certain someone for two weeks."

The argument escalated, words tumbling out faster and sharper, a rhythm Ash knew all too well. The air shimmered with their conflicting energy—his mother's smoky essence swirling in icy tendrils, her voice cutting and cold, his father's copper mesh flaring into a deep, volcanic red pulsing with anger.

Then something unexpected happened. Their colors, so starkly different, clashed violently at first, each trying to overpower the other. But instead of one dominating, they began to swirl together, their boundaries blurring. Slowly, they mixed—a storm of copper and smoke twisting into something unrecognizable yet strangely cohesive.

Ash froze, his breath caught in his chest. He'd never seen anything like it before. Their argument kept escalating, and Ash didn't want Lily to witness it.

"Lily," he whispered firmly, glancing at her, "go back to your room. I'll handle this."

Lily's eyes widened in disbelief. "But—"

Ash cut her off with a gentle but resolute shake of his head. "Lily, please. Go."

Lily hesitated, but seeing the determination in Ash's expression, she nodded quietly. "Okay," she whispered, disappearing down the hallway without another word.

Now, standing there, Ash felt uncertain about how to intervene. The atmosphere was heavy and uncomfortable. He took a deep breath, then made the decision to step in.

He walked into the kitchen, his footsteps slower than usual. His parents halted their heated exchange as he entered, both turning to look at him with startled expressions.

"Ash?" His mother tried to sound gentle, but her voice was strained, "What are you doing here?"

Ash shook his head, trying to brush off the tension. "Nothing. I was just a little hungry. I thought I'd grab something to eat for myself and Lily if that's okay."

His parents quieted, the mood shifting ever so slightly.

Ash moved to the fridge, glancing inside. He noticed the eggs were running low, and there was barely any milk or bread left. His mind immediately wandered to what they would need for the day, and he took a deep breath before speaking again.

"Dad?" He turned to his father, who was still visibly startled by his presence. "Can you take me to the store this evening? We're running out of food."

His father blinked, surprised by the request, but nodded slowly. "Of course."

Ash smiled, feeling a wave of relief wash over him. "Great. I'll whip up an omelet for you guys, too. How about you wait in the living room or wherever you're comfortable?"

Both of his parents looked equally surprised by his suggestion, but after a long pause, they slowly moved to comply, retreating from the kitchen without another word.

Although the feeling of unease lingered, Ash had done what he could to bring some calm. He set to work, gathering the ingredients for breakfast, his thoughts still crowded with the argument he'd overheard. The tension between his parents felt like a huge obstacle, but he pushed it aside for now. He would handle it later.

Before long, breakfast was ready. Ash carefully set the table, arranging everything neatly as he called out, "Lily! Mom, Dad! Breakfast is ready!"

It had been so long since they'd shared a real meal together, like a family. But as they gathered around the table, the silence in the air was deafening. Ash felt the strange gap between them—the space where laughter and warmth once flowed freely now felt stiff and unfamiliar, as if they were all just going through the motions, unsure of what to do next.

As Ash's eyes moved around the table, he saw the shift in the air—the collective discomfort of the family made the essence flicker like a low storm cloud hanging overhead. The edges of their individual essences merged and turned a sickly moss green, like damp condensation creeping slowly down the window of a forgotten room. His mother's smoky haze blended with his father's copper, and even Lily's calm blue tinged with the unsettling green.

The room felt heavier, with a low, steady pressure hanging over the meal like it was about to rain down on them. Ash felt a tightness in his chest, the urge to act, to try and shift the atmosphere somehow.

He moved instinctively, helping Lily with the eggs, bread, and milk, though the silence still pressed down on him like a weight. His father sat there, silent, distant, a far cry from the man who used to be a constant presence at the table. Ash glanced at his dad and then back at the fogged, dripping air around them, trying to find a way to break the stillness.

Deciding to take a small step, Ash handed his father the mug filled with coffee, offering a hesitant smile. "Dad, I tried to make coffee. I don't know if it's supposed to look like that. How about you try it?"

His father seemed surprised as he sipped from the mug. Ash watched carefully, waiting for a reaction. His father's voice was hoarse when he spoke. "It's good." He gave a small nod, but Ash saw the shift in his father's essence—a brief spike of dark green, signaling that the taste was likely far from desirable.

For the first time, Ash felt that he accurately deducted what the flicker meant. Ash kept his tone light. "I'll make it better next time, I promise." It felt like a small thing, something he could control—something to help ease the distance.

Turning to his mother, Ash smiled gently. "Mom, I thought some warm milk with honey might be good for you. It's good for your stomach."

His mother looked at him, surprised by the gesture. "Thank you."

As Ash passed her the cup, a small warmth seemed to fill the space, and though the moss-green essence didn't completely disappear, it eased just a little, as if the cloud overhead had lifted just enough to allow a little sunlight to peek through.

They ate in silence, the only sounds being the clinking of utensils and the occasional murmur. When breakfast ended, the spell of normalcy shattered, and Ash's mother stood and headed back to her room without a word. Their father was quieter than usual, too, retreating into the living room. Ash watched him go before turning to Lily. "Let's get ready for the store," he said, feeling the weight of the day still hanging over him.

Their father eventually drove them to the supermarket. The three of them moved quickly, gathering only what was necessary; neither Ash nor Lily was interested in straying down the aisles for things they didn't need.

Their father paused in the cereal aisle, picking up a box of Count Chocula, a brand they used to love. "How about this? You guys like this, don't you?" he asked, trying to break the monotony with a small offer.

Ash's stomach churned at the sight of the cereal, a reminder of the days when their mother had stopped making meals for them, and they were forced to eat chocolate cereal day after day because there was nothing else.

He shook his head quickly. "No, thanks," Ash replied quietly, glancing at Lily, who nodded in agreement.

"We need to get cheese, tomatoes, cucumbers, lettuce, and sausages," Ash continued as he focused on what really mattered.

Lily piped up, "Oh, and we need some household items, too. Toothpaste, shampoo, body wash..." She added the last bit without hesitation, as if the routine of gathering necessities was second nature now.

Together, they worked seamlessly, gathering everything they needed and making their way to the checkout. Their father paid for the items, his actions subdued yet still carrying the weight of responsibility to keep things together.

On the way home, Ash couldn't shake the feeling that things were far from okay, but at least today, they were functioning. They were managing. When they returned, Ash immediately began stocking the items in the fridge, organizing them methodically as Lily helped him. It felt like a quiet kind of teamwork, even if the underlying tension still lingered.

Their father, meanwhile, seemed to retreat further into himself. He didn't join in, just quietly heading into the living room, leaving Ash and Lily to take care of the rest. The quiet between them felt like a slow-moving current, pulling them further apart while also keeping them together in some strange, unspoken way.

When they were done, they followed their father into the living room. He was sitting in front of his laptop, his focus split between the screen and a phone call. His voice was strained as he muttered, "I can't find it... I already checked the mailbox... no, it's not there..." The kids exchanged glances, curiosity piqued by his frustration.

Ash hesitated for a moment before leaning in. "What are you working on, Dad?"

His father looked up, eyes tired. "I can't go to work, so I have to check some documents on the computer. Something my colleague sent me. But it's not in the mail, and I can't find it anywhere."

Ash could see the struggle on his father's face, the way his fingers hovered over the keyboard without knowing where to land. It was rare for his father to ask for help.

"Dad," Ash began, his tone tentative yet kind. "Do you want some help?"

His father hesitated for a moment, then sighed, finally giving in. "Yeah, my colleague said he sent the file. I need to check my email, but I already checked the mailbox. It's not there…"

Ash and Lily exchanged glances, Lily's lips twitching into a smile, but Ash shot her a quick look, silently urging her not to laugh. They weren't used to seeing their father in this kind of position, and though it was a little strange, Ash didn't want to make light of it.

"Maybe I can help," Ash said, despite his nervousness. "I can take a look and see if I can figure it out."

His father nodded, clearly relieved. "Go ahead, bud. Thanks."

Ash quickly got to work, opening Chrome and navigating to Gmail. He scrolled through the most recent emails and searched the attachments. There it was. Ash clicked on the document and turned to his father. "Is this it, Dad?"

His father leaned in, squinting at the screen. "Yeah, that's it. Thanks, bud." As relief seemed to seep into his father's expression, Ash noticed a subtle change in his essence. The copper that usually marked his father's aura softened, and for a brief moment, Ash saw a flicker of the gold that had once shone so brightly.

A wave of shyness washed over Ash, but he smiled, trying to keep his tone light. "It was no problem."

After a moment of silence, Ash looked up at his father again. "Um, if it's okay with you, can we watch TV now?"

His father glanced up from the laptop, "Of course, you can watch TV. Just keep the volume low, alright?"

Both Ash and Lily nodded eagerly. "Thanks, Dad."

They grabbed some pillows and settled on the floor. Then, they pointed the remote at the TV, pressing the power button. The screen flickered to life for a moment before turning completely black. Ash and Lily froze for a moment, confused. It wasn't just the TV—the whole house had gone dark.

Ash glanced at his father, who was still staring at the black screen in disbelief.

"What's going on?" their father asked, looking bewildered.

Before anyone could respond, the sound of his father's hurried footsteps filled the room as he rushed to grab his phone. "I'll call the electricity company," he muttered, his fingers dialing quickly.

Ash and Lily exchanged glances, unsure of what was happening, but they followed their father down the hall as he spoke to the person on the other end of the line.

As soon as their father got through, the tension in his voice became apparent. "Why was our electricity cut off?" he demanded. "We've never missed a payment."

On the other end, the voice was firm yet sympathetic. "The bill for the last two months hasn't been paid. It's marked as overdue."

Ash watched as shock spread across his father's face. "That can't be right. It should have been paid." His voice grew louder, frustration beginning to seep in.

The conversation heated up as their father argued, each word clipped with mounting exasperation. Ash noticed the subtle but unmistakable shift in his father's demeanor; his copper essence darkened, transforming into a deep, volcanic red. It was a clear sign that something had snapped within him, the pressure of everything finally boiling over.

Glancing at Lily, Ash saw her wide eyes filled with worry. Before things could escalate further, he placed a hand on her shoulder. "Let's go outside, okay?" he suggested quietly. "We can finish our homework in the garden."

Lily nodded, her usual curiosity replaced by concern. Gently, Ash pulled her toward the back door, the tension in the air thick enough to cut with a knife. The garden, though quiet, offered a momentary escape from the storm inside, a fragile bubble of peace. Once outside, they settled on the grass. Ash opened his book, attempting to concentrate on his homework, though his mind wandered elsewhere.

Behind them, the house resonated with the sound of their parents' raised voices, caught in a fight that Ash feared he couldn't help settle this time. The garden felt like their sanctuary, protecting them from the chaos within.

***

Sunday morning arrived with little change. His parents had become distant planets, orbiting in separate corners of the universe. They barely spoke, exchanging little more than fleeting glances. His father had claimed the living room as his new domain—sleeping and eating there as if to block himself out from the world. Ash found himself treading lightly, unsure how to address the growing divide.

The electricity remained out, leaving everything in limbo over the weekend. The banks were closed, and their father couldn't pay the overdue bill. It felt like a slow-moving avalanche, everything just piling up.

Despite the tension, Ash took it upon himself to foster some semblance of normalcy. He made breakfast and set the table for Lily and their father. When the meal was ready, he grabbed a plate for his mother, knowing she might not come down after the previous day's events.

Carrying the plate upstairs, Ash knocked gently on the door. "Mom, I brought you some breakfast. Please eat when you're hungry," he called softly.

After a moment's pause, he heard her voice—low and strained. "Come in, Ash."

He opened the door and stepped inside, his heart sinking at the sight. His mother sat on the bed, surrounded by piles of bills, their edges curled as if they had been sifted through countless times. The disorganized heap stood in stark contrast to the woman who once maintained order so effortlessly. Now, she seemed smaller and quieter, lost amid a sea of unpaid notices.

As he approached, Ash placed the plate on the nightstand. Getting closer, he felt the weight of her emotions, her familiar yellow-purple essence extending like tendrils, seeking reassurance, validation—anything to hold on to in the storm.

Her voice broke the silence, filled with unspoken plea. "Don't you think I'm doing my best?" she asked, her words nearly a whisper. "I'm trying, Ash, I really am…"

Ash sat beside her, gently placing a hand on hers. He felt the tension in her fingers and the exhaustion radiating from her—both physical and emotional. While he didn't have the answers or know how to mend what was broken, he could offer comfort.

"You're doing your best, Mom," he said, looking into her eyes with the intent to reassure her, even as he struggled to understand everything. "Please don't worry so much. Rest well. Everything will be okay, I promise."

As his hand rested on hers, Ash felt a brief, almost imperceptible flicker in her essence—an unexpected flash of bright yellow that glimmered like sunlight breaking through a cloudy sky. It was brief but unmistakable, a surge of warmth and relief that swept through her aura, softening the worn edges of her exhaustion. At that moment, he realized how much his touch could influence the energy between them. His mother, too, seemed to respond, leaning into his touch, a silent acknowledgment of the love and connection they shared.

Once his mother had eaten and drifted off to sleep, Ash quietly returned to the kitchen with the empty plate. He entered, glancing at his own share of breakfast on the table. It was cold now, but it barely mattered. He forked a piece of toast, chewing slowly.

As Ash finished the cold breakfast, he heard sounds from the living room—his father's frustrated mutterings and the sharp crack of a curse. He sighed deeply and pushed himself away from the table, walking toward the living room.

When he entered, he found his father hunched over the laptop, staring at the screen with growing annoyance. The screen was dim, the battery indicator flashing red, and his father muttered under his breath, "Of course, of course, it's dead now..." His hands clenched into fists, and then he slammed one against the armrest of the couch.

Ash hesitated before stepping in. "Dad? Are you okay?"

His father tried to remain calm, but Ash could see the fatigue etched in his eyes. "This stupid thing's dead," he said, pointing to the laptop. "I can't get anything done now. Can't charge it… can't work." His voice was hoarse and tired, as if the exhaustion had seeped into his very bones.

Ash stood there for a moment, unsure of what to say. "I can help. I could take it to the neighbors to get it charged?" he offered tentatively, but his father waved him off. "It's fine. Just go to your room."

Ash lingered for a moment longer, but when his father didn't seem to need him anymore, he retreated to his room.

***

As the sky outside deepened into evening, the house grew quieter, more still. Ash had just settled down in his room when he heard a soft knock at the door. It creaked open, revealing Lily standing outside, her wide eyes shimmering in the dim light.

"I'm a little scared in the dark," she said quietly, her voice small.

Ash immediately stood up, concern flashing across his face. Of course, Lily would be scared. The house had felt strange lately, the shadows stretching long across the walls, and with the electricity still off, everything seemed a little too quiet.

"Did you sleep okay yesterday?" he asked.

Lily nodded, but hesitation lingered in her eyes. "Yes, but I don't think I'll be able to tonight. Can I sleep in your room, big brother?"

Ash noticed faint streaks of electric purple pulsing irregularly like a heightened heartbeat, an indicator of Lily's fear. He smiled softly and motioned for her to come in. "Sure, you can sleep here. It's okay."

Lily's face brightened, relief washing over her as she climbed into his bed, tucking herself in. Ash covered her with thick blankets before sitting on the edge, watching as she quickly drifted into a peaceful sleep. Her breathing evened out, and the tension in her face faded, making Ash feel better, as if he was doing something right. He sat back in his chair, his mind wandering back to everything that had happened lately.

His family was unraveling in ways he couldn't fix, but there were tiny moments that gave him a sense of purpose. He knew he couldn't take it all on himself, but he couldn't just sit back either.

He pulled out his journal and began writing, noting the changes he'd observed in his parents' essences—the copper-red that flared up when his father was angry, the yellow-purple haze that surrounded his mother when she felt upset or sought validation. He knew it wasn't something everyone could see, but it felt real to him.

"The essences change with their emotions," he wrote. "Mom's shifts when she feels uncertain or insecure. Dad's changes when he feels overwhelmed or angry. I can see it… I don't know what it means yet, but I think it's important. Maybe if I understand it better, I can help them… somehow. When their essences change like that, they seem to shut down or push me away. I don't know what to do yet, but I'll figure it out."

Ash paused, his pen hovering over the page, feeling a little thirsty. Taking a deep breath, he made his way down the stairs. The house was silent except for the occasional creaks of settling wood. He went into the kitchen and poured himself a glass of water, taking a long sip as he tried to shake the unease from his mind.

But as he set the glass down, a thought began to gnaw at him. He didn't see his father in the living room and wondered if his father had left the house again, retreating to some place where he could escape the mounting tension. Ash's heart started to beat faster as he glanced toward the front door, then out the window toward the garden. Something caught his eye; the front door of the small workshop outside, the one his father had used for years to tinker with old gadgets and broken equipment, was open.

He hadn't seen his father go out there, but Ash figured it wouldn't hurt to check. Quietly, he stepped outside, the cool night air brushing against his face as he walked across the garden to the small wooden shed. The door creaked softly as he nudged it open, revealing a dimly lit space cluttered with old tools, half-finished projects, and the faint smell of oil and metal. At first, Ash thought the workshop was empty, but then he spotted his father at the far end of the room, hunched over a workbench.

He hadn't expected to find him here, especially at this hour. His father, usually so structured and composed, seemed different in this space. The aura Ash had come to know, characterized by a certain rigidity, was now shifting in an unfamiliar way, tinged with vulnerability. The copper surged out to become like a heavy fog and the growing gray at the edges. His face appeared more tired and worn than usual, a stark contrast to the image of strength he typically projected.

Ash's throat tightened as he stood in the doorway, unsure whether to intrude or to leave his father in the quiet of his solitude. After a moment, his father glanced up, his tired eyes meeting Ash's. "What are you doing out here?" his father asked, his voice almost fragile.

Ash hesitated, standing there in the dim light. He could see the subtle cracks in his father's carefully constructed facade, the weariness that had accumulated from months of pressure, stress, and the weight of their circumstances. It was a side of his father Ash hadn't noticed before—raw and unguarded. "I was… I was worried you left again," Ash said, his voice quiet but steady. "I didn't know where you went."

His father's eyes softened for a moment, and he sighed. "I didn't leave, Ash. Just needed a little space to think. It's hard for me, too. Everything feels... off."

Ash stepped closer, his heart aching as he looked at his father, who had always been the one to keep everything together. "I know it's hard," Ash said, "I feel it too. But... I don't think we should keep pretending like everything is fine when it's not."

His father's eyes flickered with something—maybe surprise, maybe guilt—but it was gone quickly. He ran a hand through his hair, looking away for a moment, his fingers trembling slightly. "I don't know what to do anymore," his father admitted, "I feel like I'm failing you, Lily, and your mom... I don't know how to fix it."

It felt strange hearing his father speak so openly about his struggles. For so long, Ash had thought of his dad as the pillar of strength, the one who could always make things better. But now, Ash realized that his father, like him, was just trying to survive in a world that seemed to be falling apart. "We'll figure it out," Ash said as he stepped even closer.

His father looked at him, the walls around them slowly crumbling. "I'll try, son. I'll try to become a better Dad."

For the first time in a long while, the air between them felt lighter. It wasn't much, but it was enough for Ash to sense that they were finally beginning to understand each other again.

Ash nodded, feeling something shift within him, like a tiny glimmer of hope. "I'll be here, Dad. We'll make it through. Together."

As his father let out a long, weary sigh, Ash saw that the fog hadn't fully settled, but the gold that shone through felt like the sun after a long haze—a promise of a better future.

Chapter 6: Finding Cora

The early morning air was crisp, and the streets were still quiet as Ash and Lily followed their father to the bus stop. Lily was happily holding her father's one free hand, skipping in rhythmic bursts while humming a tune Ash couldn't quite place. Her joy was infectious, and even Ash couldn't help but smile seeing her so cheerful.

The shift in their father's demeanor was noticeable. Something seemed to have changed within him after their quiet conversation last night. Ash didn't know what exactly it was, but there was a renewed tenderness in the way his father moved and in how he interacted with them. Ash had woken up that morning to find his father in the kitchen, trying to make breakfast for everyone—a noble effort, though his pancakes had turned into a burnt mess.

Ash and Lily had ended up helping, and despite the disaster, they had all laughed together, sharing a moment of warmth they hadn't experienced in a long while. Now, on their way to school, Ash couldn't help but notice that his father's copper essence felt... different. Softer, somehow.

When they reached the bus stop, Ash began pulling out his tools for the day—his sunglasses and headphones. His father, who had been silent for a while, noticed the movement and frowned slightly.

"Ash, what are you doing?" he asked with a hint of concern.

Ash hesitated before responding. He wasn't used to talking about his dizziness; it was something he had been keeping to himself for a long time. "Um... I get dizzy on the crowded bus," he said, looking up at his father. "So, I wear these on my eyes and ears. It helps. I don't feel so dizzy anymore."

His father's expression softened as understanding crossed his face. "Is that so? I didn't know. I'm sorry, Ash."

Ash shook his head, smiling a little. "Don't worry about it, Dad. It's not a big deal."

His father looked thoughtful for a moment, then asked, "But don't the teachers ask about it?"

Ash shrugged slightly. "I don't wear them in class, only outside."

"You don't get dizzy in class?" his father asked.

"I do, but I'd rather not make trouble with the teachers or my classmates. It would just be a hassle," Ash replied.

His father paused, deep in thought, before nodding slowly. "I understand. I'll talk to your teachers about it and see if we can get you a pass, okay?"

Ash's eyes widened in surprise. "You'll do that for me?" His voice cracked slightly, filled with an emotion he hadn't expected to feel.

Before his father could respond, Ash impulsively hugged his father, his heart swelling with an unexpected surge of gratitude. "Thanks, Dad."

His father was visibly taken aback, unsure how to respond, but there was something tender in his eyes as he looked down at Ash. But Ash didn't mind; the words didn't matter as much as the emotion between them. It was the first time in a long while that Ash had felt like his father truly saw and understood him.

Soon, the bus came into view, and Ash let go of his father. He called to Lily, who was standing a little way off. "Let's go, Lily," Ash said, gesturing for her to come over.

Lily skipped over, waving cheerfully as she joined Ash. "Bye, Dad!" she called, her eyes bright and carefree.

Ash climbed onto the bus, feeling lighter than he had in days. As the door closed behind them, he glanced back at his father, who gave a small, uncertain wave. His copper essence had lightened to the once valiant gold, and Ash had no doubt that change was on the horizon.

***

Once they reached school, Lily went her own way, and Ash hurried to his locker. He was eager to grab his books and slip through the day unnoticed. He didn't want to bump into his usual tormentors, the group known as Raze. Every step was calculated, his heart racing with the anticipation of a confrontation he couldn't quite avoid.

But today, of all days, his locker was proving to be troublesome. The combination wouldn't click, the dial refusing to cooperate as if it had a mind of its own. Ash muttered under his breath, trying again, but the locker door stayed stubbornly closed. He could feel the seconds ticking by, his anxiety rising with every failed attempt.

Then, he heard it.

Even through the headphones on his ear and a hoodie on his head, he could hear the unmistakable sound of laughter and footsteps echoing down the hallway—Raze was coming. Ash froze, his stomach dropping, and he instinctively yanked his bag over his shoulder, abandoning the idea of gathering books and materials for his next class.

With no time to waste, he turned and bolted down the hall. His sneakers skidded against the floor as he pushed through the door to get to the art room.

He slipped inside and quickly ducked behind a row of easels, breathing heavily. The bell hadn't rung yet, and even the teachers usually arrived five minutes after the students did, so he wasn't expecting anyone to be there.

But then he heard a slight movement. At first, Ash stiffened, thinking that the Raze had followed him. His heart raced as he strained to listen, but it wasn't as loud as it usually was. This was different.

It was the subtle, almost rhythmic scratch of bristles against textured surface, the kind of sound that could easily be lost in a noisy environment but was unmistakable when heard in the quiet.

Ash peeked around the corner of the easels, and to his surprise, he discovered that he wasn't alone. Standing by the window at a little distance was a woman he hadn't seen before—an unfamiliar face with striking features and an air of quiet confidence.

She held a paintbrush in one hand, her other resting gently on the windowsill. Her dark brown eyes were wide and observant, framed by glasses that slipped just a little down her nose. A few strands of frizzy, auburn-tinted hair had escaped from the messy bun she had tried to contain them in, giving her an unpolished yet effortlessly artistic look. Though she was short and slender, she carried herself with an undeniable presence—self-assured but kind, the sort of person who commanded attention without demanding it.

Ash's breath caught in his throat as he looked at her essence. It wasn't the typical golden or copper glow he was used to seeing around people. No, hers was something entirely different—rich, earthy tones swirling together in intricate patterns, interwoven with vibrant threads of color that seemed to pulse with life. It was unlike anything he'd ever seen.

Her kaleidoscopic aura seemed to change with every breath she took—a blend he couldn't place but found inexplicably comforting. The beautiful colors seemed to whisper a tale that Ash yearned to capture on canvas.

Before Ash could pull himself together in order to speak, the woman turned, her lips curving into a smile. "Whoever's hiding back there, I know you're there. You should come out now. It's almost time for class to start. You wouldn't want to be late."

Ash got up from his place, simultaneously taking off his glasses and headphones. "I'm sorry. I just wanted to get to class quickly and get settled but slipped."

The woman seemed amused, aware that Ash wasn't speaking the whole truth. "You're Ash Winters?" she said, looking at him thoughtfully.

Ash was surprised that someone knew him; he usually kept a low profile. He nodded. "Yes. Ma'am?"

The woman smiled. "My name is Cora Hart. I am your new art teacher."

She squinted at the glasses and headphones in his hands. "You're not supposed to have those things in class," she said, straightforward yet not unkind.

Ash's heart skipped a beat, and he looked down, his panic rising. "Yeah, I don't wear them in class, just outside," he stammered.

Miss Hart raised an eyebrow as if considering something. "Do you wear them because you think you look cool?"

Ash shook his head a little too quickly. "No." He struggled to find the words, unsure of how much to reveal. Finally, he managed to say, "My eyes are just sensitive to light, and I find it easier to get through the day when I wear headphones."

There was a pause while Miss Hart studied him, her expression shifting slightly as if she'd realized something.

Ash didn't know what exactly, but it seemed to appease her. She nodded and said, "Okay. Take your seat."

Ash didn't care what had just passed between them as long as it worked in his favor. He quickly moved to a nearby desk and set his things down, feeling a strange sense of relief that this minor detail had been handled without causing a scene.

But as Ash got settled and opened his bag, he froze. His stomach sank. He remembered he had left his books and art materials in his locker. His eyes darted over to Miss Hart, and he felt his face flush with embarrassment.

Miss Hart seemed to notice the pause in his movements and looked at him with a raised eyebrow. "What's wrong?"

Ash hesitated, biting his lip. "I… I forgot to get my paint brushes," he admitted, his voice low.

Miss Hart's lips quirked up into a smile, a hint of amusement in her voice. "But I thought you wanted to be early to class? How will it help if you're early but don't have the necessary material?"

Ash shifted uncomfortably in his seat, struggling to say something, but Miss Hart chuckled softly, the sound warm and unthreatening. "It's fine," she said, reassuring, "You can use my paint brushes."

"I also forgot my book and paints…" Ash muttered, further mortified.

Miss Hart smiled, her eyes twinkling with humor. "No worries. I've got extra books and paints for emergencies just like this." She paused for a moment before adding, her tone playful but firm, "But remember, you can't keep coming to class unprepared like this. I'm kind, but not *too* kind, you know."

Ash let out a small, nervous laugh. "I'll try not to," he promised, grateful for her understanding.

Soon, the bell rang, and his classmates trickled in. By then, Ash had settled into a quiet corner next to an open window, a canvas blocking him from the chaotic energy of the other students. It was a small but precious sanctuary, a welcome escape from the buzz of activity around him.

But then, he felt a presence beside him. He turned to find Addie sitting down with a soft smile on her face.

"Why are you hiding in this corner?" she asked, amused.

Ash shrugged, his usual response to any probing questions. "I just like corners. They're more peaceful."

But as he looked at her, something caught his eye. The edges of her beautiful emerald essence seemed to wither slightly, curling into a smoky haze. It reminded him of his mother's essence when it started to fade, and he couldn't help but voice his concern.

"Is everything okay, Addie?"

She blinked, surprised, but quickly covered it with a smile. "Of course, everything's okay. Why would you think I'm not?"

A flicker of uncertainty crossed her eyes, and the smoky haze that tinted the aura around her seemed to grow more pronounced.

Ash felt a wave of unease, but he kept his voice gentle. "I just wanted to ask how you're doing. You're my good friend, and I want you to be happy."

Addie's expression softened at his words, and the smoky haze around her began to retreat just a little. She let out a light laugh, "Thanks, Ash. That's so sweet. I'm good. Don't worry."

With that, the mood shifted, and they sat in quiet camaraderie, watching as the students filled in. Before long, the class started.

"Alright, class," Miss Hart announced, her voice calm but commanding, "I'm your new art teacher, Cora Hart. I'll be filling in for Miss Anne while she's on maternal leave. Miss Anne shared with me what we'd be focusing on today—our theme is perception. How we see the world, how we interpret things differently, even when looking at the same object, the same scene."

As she spoke, Ash couldn't help but notice the gentle shimmer of green and gold weaving through her essence, a steady, calming rhythm that seemed to make the air itself feel lighter. The room, once buzzing with quiet tension, settled into a soothing stillness, like the proverbial calm before a storm.

Cora's eyes swept across the class, waiting for a response. "Can anyone give me an example of perception?"

Without missing a beat, Addie raised her hand, her voice steady. "Rain," she said, her tone thoughtful. "For some, rain is something to be avoided—an inconvenience. It's cold, it makes you muddy, it ruins your clothes. But for others, it's almost a release, a moment to let go. When it rains, it feels as if the world has softened, like you can be yourself, free of expectations. "

"Movies often depict rain as a sign of suffering, but it's also a space for intimacy, for connection. There are so many shades of it. Even in history, some saw rain as an ill omen, a sign of hardship. But for others, it was a blessing, a gift from God. It softened the earth, helped plants grow, turned barren soil into lush fields full of life," she continued.

Miss Hart smiled warmly at Addie. "Excellent, Addie. You've captured the dual nature of rain perfectly. It's a beautiful example of how something can hold different meanings for different people." She pointed out thoughtfully, "But what about you, Addie? What do *you* think rain is?"

Addie faltered, her words hesitating on the edge of her lips. The smoky haze around her essence thickened, swirling in faint, troubled tendrils. Ash felt a flicker of concern in his chest, but before she could say anything, he found his voice.

"Miss Hart, if it's alright, can I offer my thoughts?" Ash asked, a little more uncertain than usual. His words caught everyone by surprise, including Addie, who turned toward him, her brow furrowing slightly. Cora, however, met his gaze directly, a small, knowing smile curving her lips.

"Of course, Ash. It's a free discussion, after all."

Ash cleared his throat, the words tumbling out in a rush as he found his rhythm. "Rain... it's complicated. It makes you feel both good and bad at the same time. Sometimes, you don't even know what you feel—one minute, it's refreshing, and the next, it's suffocating. It's like this strange blend of sadness and pleasure, a contradiction that makes you pause and think. Even though it brings back memories of bad times, it also washes away the hurt and makes you feel lighter, like you can move on. But for me, the most beautiful thing is when the sun rises after the rain. It's like everything's been reset, atoned for, like the world gets another chance."

He finished, feeling a slight tremor in his words, but he couldn't stop the emotions that had bled into his speech. The room felt quieter now, the weight of his words hanging in the air.

Cora's gaze softened, her smile deepening with appreciation. There was an understanding in her eyes, one that felt almost personal. Unlike others who might shrink under his gaze, she held his eyes with quiet strength as if she truly saw him—not just the words he spoke, but something beyond them. Something he still couldn't fully grasp.

"That is truly beautiful, Ash," she said, her voice warm with undeniable sincerity. "You've captured the complexity of rain in a way that most people would miss. There's beauty in the contradictions, in how they make us feel lost and found at the same time. Thank you for sharing that."

The room fell silent for a moment, the class absorbing Ash's words. Then, Cora's smile widened as she looked at the class. "Now, let's do something with all of this. Today, I want you all to paint your own perception of rain. Let's see how you can translate those feelings, those complex layers, into art. What does rain mean to you?"

Her words hung in the air like a challenge, a chance for everyone to explore their own depths through paint and brush.

Ash turned to his canvas, his fingers gripping the brush lightly, and his mind full of the imagery rain had conjured within him. He began painting a bustling street at night, the pavement slick with reflected lights from neon signs and glowing streetlamps. Raindrops fell in delicate streaks, shimmering like silver threads against the dark backdrop. A crowd of people filled the scene—some clutching umbrellas, sheltering themselves from the downpour; others moved briskly without them, heads bent, hurrying with purpose.

And then, there were those who stood still, faces turned upward, embracing the cold rain with closed eyes and half-smiles as if allowing it to wash something away.

Ash worked with fluidity, his strokes carrying the rhythm of the rain itself. But it wasn't just the figures that filled his painting—he added the essence of each one. To one woman with a bright yellow umbrella, he painted a soft glow of blue and green, a calm contentment laced with hope. A man in a worn coat, head bowed, carried a deep maroon and black haze of sorrow. A child skipping through puddles radiated orange joy tinged with a spark of curiosity. Every shade told a story, every hue whispered of hidden emotions—their satisfaction, their pain, their loss, their wonder.

As Ash layered the final streaks of light onto the rain-slicked street, he felt a presence beside him.

"This is amazing," came a soft murmur.

Startled, Ash jerked his head up to find Miss Hart standing close. He hadn't heard her approach. "Miss Hart—sorry, I didn't hear you."

She smiled, her expression amused yet thoughtful. "Well, that's exactly what you're supposed to do in art class—lose yourself in your work." Her eyes lingered on the painting, her fingers lightly tapping her chin. "Your use of color is extraordinary. Each of these individuals has a different story, a different shade. You don't just see the rain as one thing or another—you see *the people*. How interesting..."

Ash swallowed, unsure how to respond, the weight of her words settling in his chest. She *had* noticed something about him. Unlike the others, Miss Hart didn't just praise his technique; she had perceived his intent, the way his vision peeled back the layers of reality to show the emotions underneath. For the first time, he wondered if his gift wasn't just a burden but something else entirely.

"Thank you," his murmured words almost lost under the patter of imagined rain.

Miss Hart's eyes never wavered from his. "Stay after class today. I have something I want to talk to you about."

Ash nodded, a flicker of curiosity sparking beneath his calm exterior.

As the sound of her footsteps retreated, Addie leaned over to peer at his painting. Her wide eyes filled with awe. "Wow, Ash. That's… amazing."

He turned, rubbing the back of his neck, a bit self-conscious. "Thanks. Yours is amazing, too."

Both of them shifted to look at Addie's canvas. She had painted a delicate butterfly, its wings a kaleidoscope of bright, fragile colors. It perched under a bellflower, sheltering itself from the rain. But the flower, heavy with collected water, was bending dangerously low. The weight threatened to collapse onto the butterfly, its beauty poised on the edge of ruin.

Ash felt a deep sadness settle in his chest as he took it in. The emotion in the painting was evident—almost tangible. He glanced sideways at Addie, noticing the smoky haze growing thicker around her. It was slowly gnawing away at the emerald sheen that surrounded her, dimming her usual vibrancy.

"Addie," he said gently, "want to have lunch with me outside today?"

A small smile tugged at her lips. "Of course. Let's do that."

The bell rang, and students began filing out of the room. Addie gathered her things and gave Ash a light-hearted wave. "See you later," she called.

"Yeah," Ash watched her leave with a concerned gaze.

When the room finally emptied, he approached Miss Hart, "Miss Hart? You wanted to talk to me?"

She turned from her desk, her expression calm but full of purpose. "Yes, Ash. I have an assignment for you. Something just for you."

Ash tilted his head, confusion furrowing his brow. "An assignment? What do you mean?"

Miss Hart's smile deepened, her eyes kind but probing. "Ash, I see something in you. Something rare. Have you ever heard of curanderos or empaths?"

He shook his head slowly. "No… not really."

Her gaze softened, her aura glowing with the warm, amber, and pink hues of a sunset. "My grandmother used to tell me stories," she began, her eyes rich with memory. "She taught me about curanderos—healers—people who see beyond the surface. Empaths who feel emotions as if they are their own. It's a gift of connection and understanding, but it's also a burden. People are often uncomfortable with those who sense what they hide from themselves. It makes them nervous. They fear being seen too clearly. That tension is part of carrying such sensitivity. But understanding your gift... learning to wield it with intention and care... that's the path of strength and healing."

Ash felt his heartbeat quicken as her words sank in, resonating with a truth he hadn't been able to name before. "So... you think I'm like that?"

"I *know* you are," Miss Hart was confident, "And I want you to look it up. Learn about what it means to carry such awareness. Because knowing yourself—truly knowing who you are—will only make you stronger. And wiser."

Ash took a deep breath, mind swirling with questions and possibilities. "Where do I even start?"

Miss Hart placed a hand lightly on his shoulder, her touch a grounding warmth. "Start with your own perception. Observe the world as you already do—but now, with intention. We'll talk more soon. And Ash?"

"Yeah?"

Her eyes twinkled. "Trust yourself. You already see more than most ever will."

Ash nodded silently, Miss Hart's words settling into a space within him that had long been searching for answers.

He stepped out of the classroom, his footsteps echoing softly in the empty hall.

As he moved through the quiet corridors, his mind spiraled around the conversation. Her words reverberated like ripples in a still pond, spreading outward, reshaping his understanding of himself.

He recalled her essence—a beautiful kaleidoscope of colors. Unlike others, who only had one, she had many. Most of the time, if Ash ever saw any color with another, they would mix to become something prettier or uglier. But maybe Miss Hart's essence was a combination of her grandmother's support—the support of a loved one.

Maybe that's what Miss Hart meant when she talked about her grandmother, Ash mused. *She was supported by stories and teachings passed down, wisdom shared from a healer's heart. Her grandmother might have been like her. People give what they've been given in one way or another. Maybe essence is shaped by those who come before us.*

He frowned as his mind circled back to himself. *But what about me?*

His footsteps slowed, and he felt the familiar swirl of emotions rise. Was his essence a thick, murky haze of copper and smoke like his mother and father?

Dark, dirty, muddy.

He might be the very essence he feared.

The thought weighed heavy on his chest, but he clenched his fists and inhaled deeply. Even if he didn't know exactly what his own colors were, even if his essence was a mess of shadows and scars, he could choose what to do with it.

Ash lifted his head, resolve settling into his heart. If learning about perception and understanding himself could help him see and heal better, he would do it.

He would learn, and he would grow.

Because even the murkiest waters could reflect light, however little.

***

At midday, the bell rang, signaling lunchtime, and Ash went to the library as always. It was his and Addie's usual place to eat and work. As he entered, he found the room was filled with the usual murmur of hushed voices and the faint scratch of pencils on paper. Addie was already seated at their usual table, her textbooks spread out in front of her. She looked up as Ash approached.

"Not here today," he said with a small smile.

Her eyebrows rose. "Not here?"

"Let's go out."

Addie blinked. "Are you sure? We have a lot of work today."

Ash nodded, his smile widening. "Addie, work can wait. Life can't."

The words hung between them for a moment. She tilted her head, studying him. "What's up with you today? You're acting kind of… different."

"Different, as in *bad*?"

She thought it over, her lips pressing into a line before she shook her head. "No. Different as in *good*. Very good. Let's go."

They left the library and found a quiet spot beneath a large oak tree outside. The branches stretched wide, casting dappled shadows on the ground as sunlight filtered through the leaves. A gentle breeze stirred the air, carrying with it the faint scent of spring blossoms.

Settling into the grass, they both pulled out their lunches.

Ash pushed his brown paper bag toward Addie with a playful grin.

She raised an eyebrow. "What's that?"

"Pancakes."

Addie laughed as she opened the bag and peered inside. "Pancakes? Are they supposed to look like this?"

Ash chuckled, shaking his head. "Not really. But it's the first time my dad, my sister, and I made them together," he said with quiet pride in his eyes. "I promise they taste better than they look."

Addie went quiet for a moment, her gaze softening. "You made pancakes with your dad and sister?"

"Yeah."

"That's… nice."

Ash watched as her emerald glow dimmed again, the familiar smoky haze beginning to swirl around her. Without thinking, he nudged the bag closer. "Seriously, try one. I guarantee it won't give you a stomachache. Already tested and approved."

Addie glanced up at him, her lips quirking with humor. "And what if I'm allergic to something?"

"Are you?"

She laughed, shaking her head. "Nope. I'm good." She reached in, tore off a piece, and popped it into her mouth. Her eyes widened. "Wow. These are actually good."

"See?" He leaned back against the tree trunk, satisfied.

She handed him her own lunch in return. "Here. Trade. I'll take yours."

"Sure," he said easily. "And if you want, I can make more sometime. It's not a problem."

For a few moments, they ate in comfortable silence, the kind that only grew between two people who didn't need to fill the space with words. Ash watched her, noticing how her essence flickered. The haze never disappeared, but her smile seemed brighter now.

He hoped Miss Hart was right. He didn't fully understand what was going on with Addie, but if being there for her, sharing a laugh, and offering his pancakes could bring even a little comfort, he was willing to try.

He *would* try.

Chapter 7: The Prism Effect

After lunch, Ash and Addie parted ways. Addie had a gymnastics competition coming up and needed to meet her coach to finalize her routine plan. Ash, on the other hand, headed back to the quiet refuge of the school library. He began to shuffle through the shelves, searching for books related to curanderos and empaths—Miss Hart's assignment. However, since he wasn't entirely sure what those terms meant, he decided to start with a dictionary.

Flipping through the pages, he found the definition of curandero: *In Spain and Latin America, a healer who uses folk remedies.* That was a good start, but it didn't explain much beyond the surface. Ash frowned, closing the dictionary and scanning the nearby shelves for more information. His fingers brushed over the spines of various titles, some familiar and others foreign. He pulled out a few books, but none held the answers he was desperately seeking.

Frustrated, he pushed them back in place and moved further down the aisle. The library was quiet, the low hum of the fluorescent lights above the only sound interrupting the peace. The bookshelves felt endless, stretching farther than he could see. After a few moments of scanning titles, he noticed a thick, well-worn book tucked between two others. The title read *Curanderismo* by Robert T. Trotter and Juan Antonio Chavira.

His heart quickened—this was it. The book looked exactly like the kind of resource he needed. Ash pulled it from the shelf, feeling its weight in his hands. The cover was faded, and the edges were worn down from years of use. He opened the book and immediately began skimming through the pages, his eyes dancing over words like healer, spirituality, and emotional remedies. The text explained how curanderos were more than just folk healers—they were intermediaries between the physical and spiritual worlds, using their unique connection to both realms to restore balance in others.

The more Ash read, the clearer the connection between curanderos and his own experiences became. These healers worked with the emotional, physical, and spiritual states of the people they helped—something that mirrored his own gift of sensing and experiencing emotions as colors.

He discovered that many curanderos had faced personal crises that deepened their empathy, making them more attuned to the needs of others. They were skilled at understanding what others couldn't articulate, offering comfort through their knowledge and unique methods.

If curanderos could see emotions and use their understanding to heal, then maybe... just maybe... the thought stirred something inside him—a spark of hope. Could he, too, learn to manage and heal the emotions around him? Could he somehow help the people he cared about, like his mother, father, and Addie?

His mind drifted back to his family, to the vivid colors he'd seen in his father's rage, his mother's sorrow, and Addie's frequent gloom. It felt as if the colors he'd witnessed in those closest to him were shifting into darker, more difficult shades. Could he reverse it? Could he change it?

Ash's mind was still swirling with possibilities as he continued down the aisle, searching for more relevant books. The idea of becoming like the curanderos he'd read about, someone who could manage and even heal the emotions around him, felt like a life-altering decision. But was it worth it?

His schedule was already packed—there was the semester project, practical and theory quizzes, exams on the horizon, and responsibilities at home. His plate was full. Was it worth adding something else to the mix, something that might turn out to be a waste of his time?

He shook his head, trying to focus on the reality of the present. It was a lot to take on, but the more he thought about it, the more the pull of helping others—and himself—became undeniable. Maybe this could be the key to understanding not only the people around him but also his own essence. He had to try, at least, right?

Soon enough, the bell rang, signaling the end of the lunch period. Ash tucked the book under his arm, making sure to check it out before heading to his next class. He'd read more at home. It wasn't like he had any free time now, but he could always squeeze in a chapter or two later that evening.

As he walked toward the classroom for his group project, his thoughts shifted back to his team's progress. The volcano and forest were coming together nicely, with the lava and harmful gases adding a realistic touch to their display. They'd even managed to make the toy building structures look half-burned, with tiny people fleeing for their lives, being evacuated and hospitalized. The entire project had come together remarkably well.

Since they needed a place to keep it safe and away from harm, they had opted for Laila's home. Ash didn't want to risk Raze seeing him with it. Jasmine was responsible for gathering the research and had no chance of bringing it home herself, so it was left in Laila's care. And neither of them trusted Connor to be careful with it so Laila's home it was.

As Ash entered the class, he spotted Connor waving at him from across the room.

"Hey, over here," Connor called, his voice cheerful.

Ash made his way over to their group and took his seat next to Connor while Laila and Jasmine sat in front of them. However, he noticed something was off—where was the teacher?

"Where's Mr. Tanaka?" Ash asked, glancing around.

Connor shrugged, glancing at the empty desk. "He was here a moment ago, but he said he had to go. Another teacher's taking his place."

Before Ash could ask who, the door swung open, and to his surprise, in walked Miss Hart. She stepped confidently into the classroom, her heels clicking against the floor as she adjusted her glasses. "Hello, class," she said with a warm yet authoritative tone. "My name is Cora Hart, but you may call me Miss Hart." She flashed a quick smile at the students, who were still processing her unexpected entrance. "Mr. Tanaka had to leave for something, so I'll be taking over your chemistry class today."

A few students exchanged confused glances, and one raised their hand. "Is he okay?" the student asked, concerned.

Miss Hart smiled reassuringly. "Don't you worry, children," she said, soothing. "Mr. Tanaka is perfectly fit and healthy. He just had some family matters to attend to. Nothing to be concerned about."

Jasmine raised her hand, seizing the moment to speak. "But Miss Hart, we were supposed to discuss our science projects with Mr. Tanaka today. Today is the last day to finalize everything before we hand in our project tomorrow for the science competition."

"I'm aware," Miss Hart replied, her expression serious but understanding. "In fact, I'm also part of the judging committee for the competition, which is why Mr. Tanaka asked me to take over for today." She glanced at the papers in her hand, which seemed to be a list of names and projects. "Now, I have the order in which all of you are supposed to present your research."

She looked up from her papers and smiled again. "Why don't we start with Group 1? Lisa, Becky, Ben, and Timmy—please come up and present your project."

As each group presented their project, Ash's mind wandered. Soon, it was going to be his group's turn to present, and there arose an issue that had never been discussed.

Ash leaned over to Connor, whispering urgently. "Hey, do you know who's supposed to present our project? We never actually talked about it." He wasn't sure if he felt more anxious about the presentation or about the fact that they had skipped over this detail altogether.

Connor shot him a confident look, his voice low but certain. "Of course, I'm going to present it."

Before Ash could respond, Jasmine turned around quickly, her voice sharp with disbelief. "Who said so? You don't even know what the material contains. I'm the one who gathered all the research—I'm supposed to present it!" Her eyes narrowed, and Ash could see the tension beginning to bubble up.

Connor's face reddened with anger. "That's not fair," he spat, standing up from his seat. "Just because I didn't participate in the research gathering doesn't mean I don't know what's going on! I can do it perfectly well."

From there, the argument escalated rapidly. Both of their voices were slowly rising, and Ash could feel the energy in the room shift as the group before them struggled to wrap up their own presentation. Laila, sitting in front of them, looked like she was about to collapse with anxiety, her body trembling as she stared at Jasmine and Connor.

Ash felt a knot in his stomach. The essence of his three groupmates clashed—bright volcanic maroon, muddy moss, and the inky despair of a deep blue. The combination felt overwhelming. They were darker, more muddled than usual, and the energy seemed to suffocate him, causing a sudden headache to throb behind his eyes. The colors twisted in his mind like a storm of emotions he could barely contain, and he had to fight the urge to step away.

It was then that Miss Hart intervened. With a steady hand, she placed herself between Connor and Jasmine, breaking the mounting tension. "Children," she said, her voice cutting through the chaos. "Calm down. Or I'll be forced to send both of you to the principal's office."

The classroom fell quiet, the storm of colors becoming tamed, and everyone seemed to breathe a little easier. Ash couldn't help but feel a sense of relief wash over him as Miss Hart managed to de-escalate the situation.

"Now, a group project is a group project," Miss Hart's gaze swept across Connor and Jasmine, who were still glaring at each other. "All of you should decide together who should present. It doesn't matter if you choose one person or go as a whole—since all of you will be getting the same marks. Why don't you try listening to Ash and Laila? Maybe they have a good idea."

Ash and Laila exchanged uncertain glances. Laila was still visibly anxious, her hands nervously wringing in her lap. She was still hesitant about being wrapped in another argument between the other two. As much as Ash wanted to remain in the background, he knew he had to take charge.

"How about we divide it up so everyone gets a turn?" he suggested, trying to approach the solution with fairness. "Laila could talk about the project objectives since she's the one who came up with the idea. Connor could explain how these objectives are reflected in our volcanic structure; I could talk about how volcanic eruptions affect the surroundings and ecosystem. Finally, Jasmine could take over the history of volcanic eruptions—detailing everything thoroughly."

At first, no one spoke. The group seemed to hesitate, considering Ash's proposal. Laila still tapped her fingers nervously. Jasmine and Connor seemed to weigh the idea carefully, the lingering bitterness of the earlier argument still settling in their chests. But slowly, the tension began to ease.

Miss Hart smiled warmly, her approval evident in her eyes. "That sounds like a fair approach. I trust you all will be able to present as a cohesive team now that you've worked out the details."

Ash couldn't help but feel a quiet sense of accomplishment. The colors had begun to settle, his headache more bearable, and gradually, peace returned as Ash's group gave their presentation.

Later that day, Ash stayed behind after class while everyone else left for the other one. Miss Hart glanced up from her desk and noticed Ash, his fingers brushing over the strap of his backpack. The classroom was nearly empty now, save for the hum of conversation drifting in from the hallway.

"Ash?" she asked, tilting her head. "What about your next class?"

Ash hesitated, shifting his weight from one foot to the other. "About the extra class, I want to take them."

Miss Hart raised an eyebrow, a flicker of surprise crossing her face before she smiled. "Well, that was fast. But before we get ahead of ourselves, have you done the assignment I gave you?"

Ash glanced down, rubbing the back of his neck. "Not completely. But I got this book about it." He reached into his bag and pulled out the book he had borrowed from the library earlier that day, placing it gently on the desk in front of her.

Miss Hart's expression shifted again, this time to genuine surprise. She picked up the book and flipped through its pages. "You really show determination."

Then she thoughtfully returned the book to Ash, "But before we continue, there's something you should know. Being a curandero isn't easy. It's not just about seeing emotions; it's about *feeling* them, absorbing them so deeply that sometimes, you forget where you end and others begin. Their joy, their sorrow, their anger—it all becomes tangled with your own until the lines blur beyond recognition. And then, there comes a moment when you try to fix everything, to heal what's broken. But when you fail—because sometimes, you will—that failure clings to you, pulling you under. Ash, I hope you can learn to separate others' feelings from your own."

Ash considered before nodding, "I understand, Miss Hart. I'll try my best."

Miss Hart waved goodbye as Ash slung his backpack over his shoulder and left the classroom. Hearing Miss Hart's words, Ash felt he was heading in the right direction. If anyone could help him better understand what he was seeing—it was Miss Hart.

Later that evening, Ash sat at the dinner table with his dad and sister, Lily, absentmindedly pushing his food around his plate while his mind lingered on the day's events. He didn't know exactly how he was affected by the emotions of others, but the more he thought about it, the more he realized how much seeing the essence of others had impacted his choices and actions.

He had spent so much time trying to block it out that he had forgotten about his own emotions. Occasionally, he would wonder what color his essence was, but it only made him feel worse. If he couldn't learn to control what he felt— how could he ever truly help his family? How could he make sense of their pain if he couldn't even understand his own?

He had just taken a bite of his food when the phone rang. Without thinking, he got up to answer it.

"Hello?"

"Hello, am I speaking to John Winters, father of Ash Winters?"

Ash immediately recognized the voice. "Miss Hart? It's me, Ash. Wait—I'll get my dad to talk to you."

He turned to the dining room, motioning for his father. "Dad, it's for you—Miss Hart wants to talk to you."

His father wiped his hands on a napkin and took the phone. Ash lingered nearby as his dad spoke, curiosity growing with every passing second.

Across the table, Lily watched the exchange with furrowed brows. She leaned closer to Ash and whispered, "What's going on?"

"Nothing," Ash whispered back. "Just some extra classes."

Lily didn't look convinced but didn't press further. When their dad finished the call, he returned to the table and looked at Ash seriously.

"Are you sure you want to do this?" he asked. "You'll have to stay an hour after school."

Ash nodded without hesitation. "It's fine, Dad. Miss Hart teaches well, and I believe I can make better progress with her as a guide."

His father exhaled, considering for a moment before nodding. "Alright then. But if you're ever late for more than an hour, you call me. Got it?"

"Got it."

Before the conversation could end, Lily huffed. "Unfair. I want to stay after school as well."

Both Ash and their dad turned toward her. "Why would you stay after school?" John asked.

Lily crossed her arms. "Well, I wanted to try out for the volleyball team after school."

John sighed, shaking his head with a small smile. "Fine. Ash, you get your extra classes, and Lily, you can try out for volleyball. But both of you must be careful and stay in touch with me. Understood?"

Both siblings nodded in unison. "Understood."

A satisfied smile spread across Lily's face as she returned to eating, and Ash felt a quiet sense of contentment settle over him. Starting tomorrow, he would finally begin to understand what essence was.

***

The next few days unfolded with Ash attending Miss Hart's color theory lessons. As he sat at his usual spot in the front, a quiet concentration filling his mind, Ash found himself increasingly drawn to the way Miss Hart explained the color wheel. She spoke about how colors balanced one another and how opposites—like red and green or blue and orange—could create harmony or tension. It wasn't just about mixing paints; it was about understanding emotional dynamics, something Ash could relate to on a deeper level.

He couldn't help but privately note how the traditional color wheel mirrored the emotional spectrum he saw in essence. The warm reds and oranges felt like the intensity of anger or passion, while the cool blues and greens seemed to soothe and calm, much like the steady, reassuring feelings of trust. The way Miss Hart spoke about these dynamics helped him translate his experiences into something more tangible, a new language that felt more natural to him with each passing day.

During a lesson on complementary colors, Miss Hart paused and glanced at Ash, noticing the way his focus seemed to wander and the subtle shift in his posture as he fidgeted with his pencil. She'd seen it before in children with ADHD, and this time, she chose to address it directly but kindly.

"Ash," she said, "do you know every human has a maximum concentration power of about 20 minutes?"

Ash stiffened at the mention of his name, startled as he wondered if she was about to scold him. His mind raced, questioning if his restlessness had finally caught her attention in a negative light.

But Miss Hart smiled, sensing his discomfort. "It's completely normal to lose focus after that amount of time. In fact, some people have a condition where they can't focus for more than ten minutes at a time. And that's okay."

Ash blinked, not sure if she was trying to make him feel better, "But… I can't concentrate on anything," he confessed, unsure how to explain his restlessness.

Miss Hart replied thoughtfully. "Try incorporating a small movement whenever you feel your attention drifting. Something subtle—like tapping your foot or adjusting your position. It might help you concentrate better. Some like to do this in a rhythmic pattern to bring back their focus."

Ash wasn't entirely convinced, but he trusted Miss Hart. Over the next week, he began practicing this method—shifting his position in small ways, tapping his fingers, or shifting his legs in a rhythm that felt almost instinctive. The movements helped him focus, but he noticed they became jerkier than he intended at times, and he struggled to keep them subtle.

One day, during his geography class with Miss Graham, his movements grew too noticeable. Ash was trying to concentrate on the lesson, but his foot tapping and pencil tapping became distracting, too obvious to ignore. Miss Graham, who had never been sympathetic to his need to fidget, was quick to call him out.

"Ash!" she snapped as she pointed toward him. "Enough with the distractions. If you keep interrupting the class, I'll be forced to send you to detention."

Ash's face flushed with embarrassment as his classmates' eyes turned toward him. "Sorry," he mumbled, but Miss Graham wasn't finished.

"Consider this your punishment," she continued with annoyance. "You'll stay after class and finish this extra assignment for disrupting the lesson."

The punishment felt especially harsh for Ash, who had only been trying to manage the overwhelming feelings around him. Unlike Miss Hart, who understood the necessity of his movement, Miss Graham seemed to dismiss it altogether, seeing only a disruption.

After the bell rang, Ash was still thinking about what had happened in Miss Graham's class as he walked to the Art classroom the following day. He walked up to Miss Hart's desk, unsure if he should say anything, "Miss Hart... about yesterday..."

Miss Hart looked up at him, sensing the unease in his words, "Yes, Ash?"

"I was trying to focus, but I couldn't help moving jerkily," he explained, feeling a rush of frustration again. "I thought it would help, but Miss Graham just... she punished me, saying I was disrupting the class."

Miss Hart hummed thoughtfully, "Indeed, that is a pickle," she tapped her fingers lightly on the desk. "But don't worry, Ash, there's no problem that can't be solved."

Ash stared at her, a little confused. "How is this something we can fix?"

Miss Hart's smile widened. "Come to art class tomorrow morning, Ash. I think we might just have a solution."

Ash nodded, though he still wasn't sure what Miss Hart had in mind. Her confidence, though, was reassuring.

* * *

The next morning, Ash entered Miss Hart's art room, hoping to get some clarity. He found her waiting for him, as always, with a calm presence that made him feel like everything might be okay. As he approached her desk, Miss Hart handed him a small, simple blue rubber wristband.

He stared at it for a moment, still unsure. "What's this for?"

"Wear it on your wrist," Miss Hart encouraged, "Pull on it when you feel like your focus is slipping or when you need to ground yourself. Just close your eyes, pull the band, and let it go. Don't think about anything else. I'm not sure if it will work, but let's give it a try."

Ash was still a little confused but decided to give it a try. He slipped the band onto his wrist, feeling its soft stretch against his skin, "Okay."

"Good," Miss Hart replied with a small nod. "Now, go and attend your other classes. If it works, great. If it doesn't, we will try again."

Ash touched the blue wristband, a tiny reminder of the tactic he was attempting, as he made his way to his next lesson. As he sat down, the familiar anxiety began to creep in. He closed his eyes briefly, took a deep breath, and gave the band a small pull, letting it snap back lightly against his wrist.

The slight sensation grounded him, pulling his focus away from the racing thoughts. For a few seconds, the chaos in his mind seemed to quiet, just enough for him to refocus. The pressure that had been building inside his chest loosened slightly, and his breathing steadied. It was like a small pocket of calm in the storm.

The noise of the classroom was still there, but somehow, it felt less suffocating. His usually racing mind was now only buzzing lightly with distractions rather than feeling like an overwhelming tidal wave.

His fingers drummed on the desk nervously, and his eyes flickered around the room. That's when he noticed something that made him hesitate: several girls around him were wearing similar rubber bands, brightly colored ones in shades of pink, lavender, and yellow. It struck him that they were all subtly pulling on their wristbands during the class, just as he had.

Ash's face flushed a little, feeling suddenly self-conscious. The band felt foreign on his wrist, not quite like something a boy should wear. But that didn't matter if it helped him. Also, since it was an everyday accessory that everyone used, the teacher wouldn't mind. With that small reassurance, Ash focused on the lesson.

During lunchtime, Ash sat in his usual corner of the cafeteria, the one spot he'd carefully chosen to be close enough to see everything but far enough from the chaos to avoid being swallowed by it. The buzz of essences, the clatter of trays, and the constant shuffle of feet created pressure on his chest, but from his vantage point, he could filter it. It wasn't perfect, but it was manageable.

He pulled out his notebook, flipping past the earlier sketches of quick color experiments—splashes of blue and yellow that felt like chaos and calm. He glanced around, letting his eyes drift over the sea of students, taking in the colors that seemed to pulse and swirl around them like invisible auras.

At the far end of the cafeteria, the Raze's table sat like a volatile storm. His eyes caught the reds, angry and sharp, pulsing with an intensity that almost made his heart race. They didn't even need to speak for him to feel the unease— they just radiated it. Ash's fingers moved quickly over the paper, sketching jagged lines that echoed the sharpness of their auras.

"I swear if she doesn't shut up about the project—" Nate's voice broke through the hum of the cafeteria, his words low but laced with irritation. The red in his aura flared a jagged streak that cut through the tension around the table.

"Let it go, man," Jackson flicked a piece of his sandwich across the table. "She's just trying to get us to do the work. But seriously, can we just get this over with?"

The energy around them pulsed with discontent as they exchanged terse words, their body language sharp, avoiding eye contact but clearly locked in a silent battle for control. The reds at the table deepened, almost seeming to vibrate with frustration. His hand moved faster across the page, trying to capture the feeling of aggression that hung heavy in the air.

Nearby, the drama club table was an entirely different world. Here, the colors swirled in a chaotic dance of deep purples, oranges, and greens, mixing with tinges of yellow as people shifted between performance anxiety and creative energy. The aura around each person was fluid, constantly changing as their conversations bounced from one topic to the next, sometimes dramatic, sometimes thoughtful, always in motion.

"I'm just saying, if I mess up my monologue in front of everyone, I'll—" Hanna broke off mid-sentence with her messy bun and neon green glasses. Her essence flickered nervously in a wash of pale yellow.

"Relax, Hanna, it's just a class performance," Matt reassured her, giving her a smile as he scribbled in his notebook, his essence a warm orange, flickering with bursts of creative energy. "You're going to do fine. We've all got your back."

Hanna's smile was uncertain, but she nodded, her yellow aura softening slightly as she took a deep breath. "Thanks, I guess… It's just that opening night stuff always gets to me."

Ash smiled faintly, capturing the interplay of colors with softer, curved lines in his notebook. He could almost feel the flow of energy as it mixed between them like they were all feeding off each other's creativity and stress. The Raze was similar in the way that their essences were feeding off of each other's negative energy.

Ash jotted down the last few details in his notebook, feeling the page come alive with the colors and emotions of the moment. He had learned something new today—not just about the colors, but about the way emotions connected people, sometimes lifting them and sometimes pulling them down.

Excited, Ash couldn't wait to show Miss Hart his progress. He felt a spark of anticipation at the thought of explaining his new understanding of emotional energy. But as the bell rang, signaling the end of lunchtime, it hit him— his next class was Miss Graham's. A cold rush of tension settled over him as he started walking to his next class.

***

Ash sat up straighter, trying to keep his movements subtle, trying to be invisible. Miss Graham had a way of making him feel like she was always watching, waiting for him to slip up. The walls of the classroom seemed to close in on him, the hum of students around him blending into an almost overwhelming buzz.

As the lesson began, Ash's mind wandered, his thoughts slipping back to his notebook, to the colors, to the way emotions flowed like rivers. But it didn't take long before he felt that familiar restlessness. His foot tapped, and his fingers twitched. He grabbed the wristband, flicking it lightly to keep his focus, but something snapped. The rubber stretched too far, and there was a loud, unexpected *snap*.

The noise seemed to echo in the silence of the classroom. Ash's heart skipped a beat. He looked up, only to find Miss Graham's piercing gaze locked on him as if she'd been waiting for him to do something wrong.

"What was that?" she demanded.

Ash froze, suddenly aware of the eyes on him, "Nothing, Miss Graham. Just something to help me focus on the lesson."

"It didn't sound like nothing," Miss Graham retorted, her eyes narrowing. She grabbed his hand and saw what it was, "A rubber band to help you focus? Do you take me for a fool, Ash?"

Ash's frustration started to bubble up. He wanted to say something, but Miss Graham scoffed. "Take it off. Now. If you don't, you're getting detention."

Ash clenched his jaw, refusal bubbling up in his throat. The stares of his classmates, the looming dread of Miss

Graham's disapproval—it was too much. But he didn't want to make things worse. Sighing, Ash pulled off his wristband, and Miss Graham snatched it from his hands, continuing with the lesson.

Without it, Ash's focus drifted again. He wanted to move, but he was sure Miss Graham would point it out. So, he took out his notebook, hoping the sketching would help him filter the overwhelming emotions in the room. He made sure to keep it hidden beneath the desk, out of sight from Miss Graham.

With swift, almost subconscious movements, he began drawing the jagged lines of her aura—the dark, sickly green and the deep black that seemed to pulse with negativity. The colors on the page mirrored the discomfort that had started to settle in his stomach. He focused on the lines, hoping they would bring him some clarity, some release.

It wasn't long before Miss Graham's sharp voice cut through his concentration again.

"Ash," she snapped. "How dare you draw during my class?"

His eyes darted up, and her steely gaze met his. He knew what was coming next. A sense of defeat washed over him as she handed him a detention slip. The room seemed to close in on him, and he could feel the sharp heat of the shame creeping up his neck.

When the class finally ended, Ash let out a breath he hadn't realized he'd been holding. He packed up his things slowly, his shoulders tense. But as he stood, he felt a hand on his arm. Addie stood behind him, looking at him with concern.

"Ash, what's going on with you these days? I hardly see you anymore," she asked quietly.

Ash hesitated. He hadn't told Addie about the extra lessons with Miss Hart. He hadn't told anyone except for his family, really. But Addie was a good friend, so he smiled. "Nothing, just a little busier."

They walked together toward their next class, the atmosphere between them lightening as they exchanged small talk. Ash felt a little more at ease as they neared Miss Hart's art room, the sanctuary he'd grown to appreciate. When they reached the door, he revealed, "I've been getting extra lessons from Miss Hart."

Addie's expression shifted instantly. Her aura, previously a calm emerald green, started to darken, swirling with smoky tendrils that hinted at something deeper. Ash felt the shift immediately and wondered what he had said to cause it.

Ash's mind spun, trying to find a way to ease her discomfort. "How about you join us after class? I'm sure Miss Hart wouldn't mind."

Addie hesitated for a moment before shaking her head. "I'm fine," she said, but her essence felt distant, even if her smile remained. "I have gym after this, so I can't join you."

Ash wanted to appease her, so he suggested, "Then, let's meet every day for lunch? We can paint together."

The smoky haze around Addie's aura lightened just a little, the tension in her expression easing. "That sounds good."

Ash felt a small sense of relief. Her aura seemed brighter again, lighter than it had been moments before.

They both entered Miss Hart's art room together. Ash settled into his seat, and Addie sat next to him.

"Today, we're going to explore Mexican folk art symbolism," Miss Hart began.

She moved around the room as she explained, "It's a beautiful tradition, deeply rooted in emotions and stories. The colors and the patterns carry a deeper meaning. They represent a way of seeing the world with heightened sensitivity, just like some of you do with your own unique perception."

Ash felt intrigued by what Miss Hart was saying. It made him feel as though the essence he was familiar with wasn't a foreign concept at all. They were part of a tradition of sensitivity and perception that had existed long before him.

Miss Hart continued, explaining how certain colors in Mexican folk art symbolized specific emotions and life forces. "For example, red can represent passion or danger, while green is often associated with hope and renewal. The way these colors interact in a piece tells a story. And I think you all have the ability to understand that, especially when you use your unique perspectives."

Then, Miss Hart encouraged everyone to experiment with different mediums, reminding them that art was about exploration, not perfection. Ash picked up a set of watercolors and began mixing them, letting the colors swirl together on his paper. The fluid nature of the paint seemed to match his mood—a quiet, flowing energy that helped him process the emotions he'd been sensing throughout the day.

He tried to focus on his feelings of relief and peace, letting the watercolors capture the softness that had come over him after listening to Miss Hart. The colors blended beautifully, each stroke representing the calm he had been searching for.

His brush moved in fluid strokes, capturing the peaceful sky outside the window. The soft blue hues of the sky and the bright, cheerful rays of the sun shining through the glass seemed to embody the calm he felt. But as his gaze shifted back to the classroom, he noticed a shift in the energy— tension simmering beneath the surface of the students' movements and conversations.

He paused, switching to charcoal. The contrast was stark. The fluid, peaceful strokes of the watercolor gave way to sharp, jagged lines as he captured the discomfort and restlessness in the room. He outlined the faces of his classmates, each one reflecting a different shade of anxiety or frustration. The charcoal highlighted the tension in the air, transforming the classroom into a complex landscape of emotions.

By the end of the class, he took a step back and looked at his work. For the first time, he had captured the true emotional undercurrent of his classmates that flowed beneath the surface. The sunlight pouring into the room still bathed everything in a soft glow, but the students, with their subtle shifts and unspoken feelings, had come to life in a way that felt true.

Miss Hart, who had been watching from the corner of the room, came over as the class ended. She looked at his drawing for a long moment, her eyes studying it intently. "This is... incredible," her voice was soft with admiration. "It feels like you're channeling the whole room's energy."

Ash smiled, a quiet pride swelling within him. "It just felt like I was tapping into something, you know?"

Miss Hart nodded, her eyes lighting up. "Exactly. It's like you're using your intuition, not just your technique. Art isn't just about what we see—it's about how we feel and what we can express through that."

Ash thought about the way Miss Graham had dismissed his need for movement and his attempt to explain that it helped him focus. He had felt frustrated then, trapped by her rigid expectations. But now, as he stood in the art room with Miss Hart, he realized that intuition and movement—whether in his art or his life—were just as valid as anything else. His ability to process emotions through art, to create something meaningful from his feelings, was his strength. And that, Ash decided, was what truly mattered.

Chapter 8: Marcus's Storm

Ash left Miss Hart's classroom with her words still echoing in his mind. The exhaustion of the day clung to him, but it was a good feeling—as if he was close to understanding the essence. He traced his fingers along the edge of his notebook as he walked, lost in thought.

The hallways were mostly empty after school, with occasional footsteps echoing in the distance. Not expecting to run into anyone, Ash had taken off his glasses and headphones, letting the quiet settle over him. He was about to turn a corner when something—or someone—slammed into him.

The impact knocked him off balance, sending him sprawling onto the cold tile floor. A sharp jolt of pain shot up his arms as he landed hard, his breath escaping in a sharp gasp. His notebook slipped from his grasp, pages fanning out like fallen leaves. For a moment, everything blurred, and then he looked up.

A sharp glare met his gaze, piercing and unrelenting—and behind it—red. Not merely red but volatile, chaotic, blistering in its intensity. The essence radiated outward in jagged, erratic waves, searing into Ash's vision like molten fire. His head throbbed instantly, a deep, punishing ache blooming behind his eyes.

His stomach twisted violently, and he nearly doubled over from the intensity of the sensation. He gripped the floor, trying to steady himself, but the pressure felt suffocating. The room swayed around him, and the chaotic energy pressed harder, making it almost impossible to breathe.

The kid in front of him was Marcus Ortiz, the new transfer student. He was stout and broad-shouldered, bigger than most boys his age, with dark hair that hung over his eyes. Dressed in stylish black, he had an intimidating presence—serious-faced, his expression set in a near-permanent look of defiance. A look of disgust twisted his face as he clicked his teeth, and Ash felt the sting of his gaze like a physical blow.

"Watch it, halfwit. Are you blind?" Marcus sneered, his voice dripping with disdain before he turned and walked away, leaving a trail of bitterness in the air.

Ash's heart pounded. All he could focus on was the unbearable throbbing in his head. "What in the world was that?" he thought. The essence felt so emotionally charged, as if it created a barrier around Marcus. It pulsed and twisted, a violent energy that was almost tangible. Ash had seen red before, even on his father, but never like this—never so intense, so *raw*. It was like an unfiltered storm, tearing through everything in its path.

What in the world had happened to him?

The question still reverberated in Ash's mind, but there was no answer—only the thrum of his pulse and the lingering echo of that suffocating, red-hot aura. He barely noticed the footsteps approaching, too lost in his own thoughts.

"Ash? Hey, you okay?" Lily's voice cut through his haze. She had just finished her gymnastics practice, her athletic bag slung over her shoulder.

He blinked, trying to refocus, and looked at his sister. "Yeah, just… a weird moment, that's all."

Lily gave him a scrutinizing look, but she didn't push. Instead, she smiled softly, extending her hand, "Come. Let's go home." Ash nodded, taking her hand, and they walked together in silence, heading back home.

***

When they reached their house, Ash moved to prepare dinner, but his father, John, noticed something was off. As Ash entered the kitchen, he glanced over at him with a raised eyebrow. "What's up, Ash?"

Ash didn't answer immediately, too distracted by the previous events. But then John reached out, lightly patting his head. "You... you have a fever," he said, surprised.

Upon hearing that, Lily turned with a frown. "You had a fever? Why didn't you tell me?"

Ash waved a hand dismissively. "No, I'm fine. I just need to sleep, and it'll go away."

John, however, wasn't buying it. "Nonsense. You need to rest."

Ash hesitated, then glanced toward the kitchen counter, "But what about dinner?"

"Don't worry, we'll order something today," John said with a reassuring smile. "Maybe some nourishing soup for you. Let's get you to bed."

Reluctantly, Ash followed his father upstairs to his room. His fever still lingered, a dull ache throbbing in his head, but he kept telling himself it would pass soon.

***

The next day, his fever still clung to him, and he had to take the day off from school. John stood by his bed, gently taking Ash's temperature with the thermometer. After a moment, he gave a slight frown. "100.3°"

Ash blinked, unsure if that was good or bad. "Will I be able to go to school today?" he asked, his body sore from the high temperature.

John shook his head in mild disappointment. "Sorry, buddy. You can't go to school like this. I'll call your teachers and let them know."

Ash flopped back on his bed with a dramatic thump, "I hate getting sick."

John sympathized, pulling the blanket up to cover Ash fully. "I hate it too."

Lily looked at Ash with concern in her eyes. Her brow furrowed, "Are you sure you're okay?"

Ash managed a weak smile but shook his head, "I'm fine, but you should stay away from me," he said quietly. "I don't want you catching a cold from me."

John agreed, giving his daughter a reassuring look. "Lily, you should keep your distance for now."

Lily pursed her lips but nodded, "I'll tell Miss Hart that you couldn't attend the extra class today because you were sick."

"Thanks," Ash said, smiling faintly at his sister.

With that, Lily and John left the room, closing the door quietly behind them. Ash let his eyes drift shut, the warmth of the blanket and the faint sounds of his family moving around the house lulling him into a deep sleep.

Fortunately, his temperature had cooled down by night. John suggested he stay home for an extra day, but Ash, stubborn as ever, shook his head.

"No, I'm better now. I can go. The day after tomorrow is Saturday anyway, so it's fine."

John gave him a knowing look but didn't push the matter further. "Alright, but if you feel off, don't push yourself."

Ash nodded, though his mind was already wandering. He couldn't shake the memory of Marcus Chen and the intensity of that red essence. Despite the lingering fever and the strange encounter, he was determined to push through the day. Whatever it took, he would manage.

***

The next morning, Ash made sure to keep his glasses and headphones on as he prepared for school. He took his ADHD medication, hoping it would help him focus better, and hurried to his first class of the day—mathematics with Miss Cecilia. He tried to mentally prepare himself for the day ahead, but his thoughts kept drifting back to Marcus's chaotic red aura.

As soon as he entered the classroom, Ash felt a wave of hesitation. He was about to take his glasses off, but when his gaze swept over the room, he froze.

There, sitting at the back of the class, was none other than Marcus Chen.

Ash's stomach dropped at the sight of him. He didn't want to look at the guy at all—not after what had happened. So, he chose the furthest seat he could find—the front row, closest to the classroom door. It was the last place he wanted to be, but at least it meant he wouldn't have to face Marcus directly.

Ash slipped off his glasses and headphones, trying to settle in. But even though he sat so far from Marcus, he could still sense it—that red essence. It was like a pulsing presence in the air, too tangible for him to ignore, like the color was bleeding into everything around it.

As Miss Cecilia started to write questions on the board, Ash couldn't help but sneak a glance over his shoulder, his eyes involuntarily drawn to Marcus.

Even though he sat far away, the essence was still overwhelming. When Ash was about to look away, something caught his attention in the midst of that chaotic red aura: a fragment of something darker, more substantial. It was a deep, suffocating grey that coiled protectively around the red.

Ash's breath caught—he had seen this before.

It was exactly like the grey similar to his father's aura during moments of despair—when his father's emotions had been at their most fragile and uncontrollable, particularly that night in the tool shed.

Ash had learned that the grey core was a vulnerable, painful side of someone, often protected by various emotions. His father's essence was often copper, and it only became red when he was angry, which was a rare event. Maybe because he was mature and older than Marcus, but still, Marcus's essence seemed more hostile. It was like a storm protecting an unyielding core, a force completely unlike the gentleness Ash had seen in his father's aura.

But why?

The class was quiet except for the scribbling of pens on paper and the low hum of the clock ticking away. Ash was still lost in his thoughts, trying to piece together what he had sensed in Marcus's essence.

"Ash," Miss Cecilia's voice cut through his thoughts, pulling his attention back to the classroom. "Ash, come solve this problem on the board."

Ash blinked, his gaze snapping toward the front of the class. He nodded, standing to walk up to the board. His hands were steady as he approached the equation, his mind automatically shifting gears. He solved the problem quickly, and the numbers and symbols aligned perfectly in his mind.

When he finished, he turned to face Miss Cecilia, who nodded approvingly. "Good job, Ash. But you should focus on the class more."

"Yes, Miss Cecilia," he replied, returning to his seat.

Then, the teacher turned toward the back of the class, where Marcus sat. "Marcus," she called, "You're a new transfer student, right?"

Marcus glanced up, his expression unreadable. He didn't respond, his gaze lingering on the desk in front of him, his posture stiff and defiant.

Miss Cecilia sighed, clearly losing patience. "Come on, Marcus. You're here to learn. Solve the next problem on the board."

Marcus didn't move. He remained seated, his arms crossed, his gaze fixed on the desk as if the outside world didn't exist.

Ash didn't look back, but he felt a strange tension building in the room as if the air was thickening and ready to crack open. Miss Cecilia, now visibly irritated, walked toward Marcus's desk, her shoes clicking on the floor with each step. "Marcus," her tone was sharp as she said, "Get up. Come solve the problem."

The class fell silent, waiting, watching. Ash could feel the energy shift—his attention snapping back to Marcus, almost against his will. His aura was different now. It pulsed, erratic, chaotic—like a storm building.

The eruption came as Miss Cecilia reached out to touch Marcus's shoulder. He shot to his feet, his chair scraping loudly against the floor. His face was twisted in anger, his fists clenched at his sides. The red in his aura surged violently, splintering into jagged, dangerous spikes that seemed to tear at the air itself. Ash could feel its heat radiating even from the front row. His head throbbed, the intensity of the chaos nearly overwhelming him.

"Don't touch me!" Marcus's voice rang out, raw and furious, the words cutting through the tension like a knife. The red essence flared as if to match the rage in his voice, swirling around him in violent streaks of color.

Miss Cecilia froze, eyes wide with surprise, but she didn't back down. "Marcus, this isn't the way—"

"Mind your business!" Marcus snarled, seething with frustration. His eyes locked onto Miss Cecilia, his glare almost challenging. "I'm not doing your stupid problem."

Ash felt the shiver of Marcus's pain as it radiated in his essence. It was a raw, exposed emotion, shielded by layers of anger and defiance, but its core was clear to Ash.

The classroom was still. No one dared to move. Miss Cecilia simply stood there, at a loss for words, her hand still hovering midair.

Marcus, his aura still crackling with anger, turned sharply on his heel and stalked out the door. His steps were heavy, filled with frustration. His red essence flickered in the air, violently pulsing like it was constricting Ash's chest.

Miss Cecilia made a move to follow, but she hesitated, her feet frozen in place. Her hands trembled slightly at her sides, her face conflicted. It was clear she wanted to check on him to ensure things didn't escalate further, but something held her back.

Ash, on the other hand, felt an overwhelming sense of concern stirring in him. Even though he didn't know Marcus personally, thinking back to his father's loneliness that night, Ash felt the similarity between the two—that raw vulnerability hidden behind layers of anger and pride.

And so, before he could stop himself, Ash stood and moved toward the door, his body already acting on the impulse that had been building in him for days.

Miss Cecilia looked over, her eyes widening in surprise. "Ash, wait!"

But Ash didn't stop.

He ran out the door just as Marcus was about to turn the corner. His heart was racing, his breath already unsteady as he followed Marcus down the hallway. The air around him crackled with heat, a tangible force that was painful to his senses.

"Marcus, wait!" Ash called out, his voice cracking slightly. He wasn't sure what he was doing, but it felt like something that pulled at his chest like a magnetic force.

Marcus spun around, his face twisted in irritation, his glare sharp enough to cut through steel, "Stop following me."

Ash's breath hitched. His head was pounding from the intensity of Marcus's essence, but he couldn't bring himself to back down. Something in him refused to let it go.

"I'm not… I'm not trying to—" Ash started, but before he could finish, the words tumbled out without thinking. "It must be hard, feeling so alone…"

The moment the words left his mouth, he immediately regretted them. The air around Marcus seemed to ripple with even darker energy, the red aura flaring out of control, spiking dangerously as Marcus spun to face him. His eyes were wild, filled with a fury that burned through Ash's very soul.

"Mind your own business!" Marcus snarled, his voice low but seething with anger. "And stop looking at me like that."

Ash froze in place, Marcus's words hitting him like a physical blow. The air between them felt charged as if any wrong move could trigger something volatile. But despite the searing intensity of Marcus's rage, there was something else simmering beneath the surface.

Ash's chest tightened, and for a moment, he didn't know how to respond. The heat of Marcus's essence was pushing in from all sides, but he didn't step back. He couldn't. Something inside him made him stay, even if it hurt.

"I'm sorry," Ash whispered. His breath was shallow, and his vision blurred, the emotions in the air growing harder to bear. He wanted to say more—something, anything—that might make Marcus understand. But words felt so small.

Marcus didn't wait for him to say anything else. He turned sharply on his heel again, storming off down the hallway. Ash watched him go, his own heart sinking, the sting of the confrontation still fresh in his chest. He didn't know if he'd helped or if he'd only made things worse. But one thing was clear—Marcus was hurting deeply, and Ash wasn't sure how to reach him.

***

The week following the confrontation felt heavy for Ash. He couldn't shake the memory of Marcus's angry outburst or the intense energy that had swirled around them both. Marcus seemed to deliberately avoid Ash each day—never making eye contact in the hallways, keeping his distance in shared classes. It was as if Marcus was trying to make himself invisible, hiding behind his walls of anger and discomfort. And Ash could feel it—the way Marcus's aura flickered with sharp spikes of hostility every time he came near, even if Marcus wasn't looking directly at him.

While Ash had tried to respect the distance, it didn't make the situation any easier. It only deepened the confusion and unease he felt. He had seen Marcus's pain, and it gnawed at him—making it difficult to ignore. But the more he tried to make sense of it, the more he realized that his instinct to reach out, to help, might not be the right approach. Sometimes, seeing the pain wasn't enough; sometimes, it was better to leave it alone.

During an extra class with Miss Hart, Ash found himself unable to concentrate on the material. His thoughts kept drifting back to Marcus, wondering if he was okay and if he had made things worse by speaking up. He had to ask someone, and Miss Hart was the one who understood him best.

"Miss Hart," Ash started hesitantly after class, "I've been thinking a lot about Marcus… and the confrontation last week. I feel like I did something wrong."

Miss Hart raised an eyebrow, setting down her papers with a soft sigh. "What makes you say that, Ash?"

"He had a fight with Miss Cecilia, after which I followed him to help but accidentally pointed out his loneliness. I tried to reach out, but... I think I made things worse," Ash confessed, running a hand through his hair. "He's avoiding me now, and I don't know what to do."

Miss Hart studied him for a moment, then spoke with gentle wisdom. "Ash, you have a beautiful gift. You can sense things about others—how they feel and what they're going through. But there's something you need to learn, something important: knowing how someone feels is fine, but confronting them about it can be intrusive. Sometimes, you can't fix what you see, and pushing someone to confront their own pain before they're ready is, well, disrespectful."

Ash blinked, absorbing her words. "But... I just want to help. I want to apologize to Marcus. I don't want him to feel so alone."

"I know you do," Miss Hart said kindly. "But it's not about what you want, Ash. It's about giving Marcus the space he needs to deal with his own emotions. If he wants help, he'll come to you. You have to wait for him to ask for it rather than forcing your help onto him."

"But what if he never asks?" Ash asked quietly, his voice tinged with frustration.

Miss Hart smiled, a small, knowing expression that made Ash feel like she was speaking from experience. "Then it's not your job to fix it. Sometimes, just being there when he's ready is enough. It's about respecting his boundaries."

Ash nodded slowly, letting her words settle in his mind. It felt hard to accept—he wanted to do something for Marcus, to make things right—but Miss Hart's words made sense. He couldn't force someone to open up. That wasn't fair.

"I understand," Ash said, his voice soft. "But... I still want to apologize to him. I just feel like he might fight me at every turn. I don't know how to do that without making him feel worse."

Miss Hart thought for a moment, and then a small smile tugged at the corner of her mouth. "How about this?" she said, her eyes twinkling with something like mischief.

Ash's curiosity piqued.

She leaned forward slightly, whispering in secrecy.

Ash considered it for a moment, then said, "I think I could do that."

"Good," Miss Hart replied, her smile widening, "And remember, sometimes the smallest gestures can have the biggest impact."

Ash left the classroom, his mind buzzing with possibilities.

***

The next morning, Ash arrived at class earlier than usual, his heart pounding with a mixture of nerves and anticipation. He clutched a card in his hand, something he had painted himself the night before. He had squeezed the image of aligned planets into a passport-sized canvas, delicate swirls of color flowing between the planets as though they were in quiet harmony. The painting was simple but meaningful, a peaceful scene that Ash hoped might reach Marcus without words.

He placed the card carefully on Marcus's desk before settling into his own. Although he felt a twinge of discomfort as he looked at the desk, he didn't let his anxiety stop him. This was just a small gesture, something that would let Marcus know that someone was there.

Soon, the class began to trickle in, and Ash tried his best to focus on his own thoughts. He couldn't help but keep an eye on Marcus's desk, waiting for the moment when Marcus would sit down and see the card.

Finally, the door opened, and Marcus walked in, his essence already sending waves of intensity through the room. The sharp, dangerous energy clung to him, making Ash tense slightly in his seat. His eyes kept flickering toward the desk, watching, waiting.

When Marcus dropped his bag on the floor and sat down at his desk, his gaze fell directly on the art card. Ash didn't dare look back at him, but he could feel the subtle shift in the air. The jagged, volatile red waves calmed just a little as if the sight of the peaceful image had defused some of the tension. Marcus hesitated for a moment, picking up the card with a quiet curiosity.

Ash held his breath, hoping Marcus wouldn't question it or toss it aside. Just as Marcus looked up at his classmates with a look of inspection, Ash quickly turned his head toward the front of the class, hoping Marcus hadn't caught him peeking.

As the class went on, Ash couldn't help but glance over at Marcus's desk again. The red essence was still present, but it wasn't as harsh, not as suffocating as it had been before. It seemed a little lighter, the spikes of anger retreating just slightly, replaced with a sort of guarded stillness.

Over the next few days, Ash found himself continuing this quiet ritual. He would arrive early to class, leaving small sketches on Marcus's desk—scenes of peaceful landscapes, quiet rivers, or distant mountains bathed in sunlight. The scenes were always simple and serene, meant to evoke a sense of calm. Ash was careful to ensure that each sketch was general enough that Marcus wouldn't feel exposed or singled out. He didn't want to force anything; he just wanted to create a space where Marcus could breathe without the weight of the world on his shoulders.

And each time Marcus discovered the sketches, Ash could sense the subtle shift in his aura. The violent bursts of anger were still there, lurking beneath the surface, but the calming effects of the artwork were beginning to take root. It wasn't a dramatic change, but Ash could feel it. There was a slight easing in the air whenever Marcus picked up one of the cards, a brief pause before the storm returned.

Ash didn't know if Marcus ever realized who was leaving the cards. He never saw any sign of acknowledgment, but the changes were there, quiet but undeniable. Marcus was still distant, still angry, but Ash had come to understand that some things took time. All he could do was continue to leave the sketches, watch for the subtle changes, and hope that someday when Marcus was ready, he would reach out if only to say thank you. Or, perhaps, to say something more.

***

Art class was next; Ash hesitated at the doorway, his eyes scanning the classroom. He was about to settle into his usual spot near the door, away from Marcus, when Miss Hart's voice called out to him.

"Ash, what are you doing? Your seat is here, isn't it?" she asked, pointing to a seat near the back corner by the window, right next to Marcus's desk.

Ash froze, caught between a desire to keep his distance and Miss Hart's gentle insistence. He looked at the seat she had pointed to, then at Marcus's desk, which felt like the last place he wanted to be near. But Miss Hart's gaze was unwavering, and Ash knew better than to argue with her when she made up her mind.

With a reluctant sigh, Ash walked over and sat in the seat she had assigned him. Addie, who was just about to sit next to him, glanced at Marcus's desk, hesitated, and then chose a seat in front of Ash, her back slightly turned from Marcus. Even though she was cautious, the lingering tension from the previous math class was still palpable.

Ash settled into his seat, trying to ignore the nervous knot forming in his stomach. He could feel Marcus's presence near him, but he kept his gaze trained on the table, focusing on the quiet hum of the room as others filed in. The soft rustling of sketchbooks, the scratch of pencils on paper—it was a familiar rhythm that helped ease the unease bubbling inside him.

Miss Hart smiled at the class as she passed by, her eyes lingering on Ash momentarily as if sensing his hesitation. But she didn't comment further, allowing the students to settle into their creative space. Ash focused on his sketchbook, fingers curling around his pencil, trying to block out the distractions and the subtle tension in the air.

Today, he decided to create a piece he had been thinking about for a while. The idea had been lingering, unexplored, and today, it seemed to demand his attention.

He began to sketch, the lines flowing easily, though his mind was still occupied by the question troubling him. The essence of people varied, shifting with emotions, with moments, with the quiet hum of the world around them. So why couldn't he see the essence of babies or toddlers?

Ash paused, his pencil lightly grazing the paper as he considered the thought. Babies, like everyone else, felt emotions—they cried when hungry or upset and laughed at something that amused them. But those emotions seemed simpler, more straightforward, and limited to only a few basic expressions. They didn't show the same intensity or complexity as adults.

But why not?

Maybe it was because they were still protected and shielded from the more overwhelming parts of life. Perhaps,

Ash thought, they didn't need to express the vast spectrum of feelings that adults did because they hadn't experienced the same emotional chaos. Their essence could be simpler, more contained, and perhaps that was why he couldn't see it. Or maybe, just maybe, their essence was a color unseeable by his eyes—a color outside the spectrum of what he could perceive.

He leaned back slightly, looking at the sketch on the page before him. It was a delicate outline of a small, folded form of a baby curled up like a shell, protective and contained. The essence within the figure was a soft, muted white because Ash couldn't bring himself to choose a color for it. He didn't know what shade it should be, what it should represent, so he left it untouched, a quiet mystery.

Around the baby's form, the surroundings were inked in dark, sweeping strokes of black. The contrast felt intentional, as if the darkness outside encroached on the fragile, pure white inside, a quiet representation of the world's complexities and the protection a baby still had, untouched by its chaos.

His pencil hovered over the final details, but something about the piece felt incomplete. As he sat there, his thoughts pressed against his chest, Ash shifted his attention toward Marcus's painting. The style was bold and powerful—there was no hesitation in the way Marcus applied the paint. The image before him was a jagged mountain, built up in thick layers of paint, dark and imposing. At the summit of the mountain stood a lone wolf howling into the darkness of a cloud-covered night. The moon, a faint hint of light beneath the heavy clouds, seemed almost unreachable, buried beneath the weight of everything above.

The emotional weight of the piece was palpable and raw. Ash couldn't help but feel a sense of understanding. There was something so honest about it, a vulnerability that Marcus rarely showed in person but poured onto the canvas. It was a longing, a quest for something that seemed impossible to attain—like the wolf searching for the moon, always out of reach.

Miss Hart stood by Marcus's desk, her eyes tracing the sharp edges of the wolf's silhouette against the heavy, shadowy clouds. She was silent for a moment, letting the piece speak for itself before finally addressing the class.

"Marcus," she said, her voice softer than usual, "this is truly remarkable. The rawness of emotion you've captured in your painting—it's not easy to put yourself out there like this. This is the kind of honesty that makes art powerful."

For the first time, Miss Hart's praise wasn't directed at Ash. The shift in focus was subtle but significant. The classroom buzzed with murmurs of admiration. Marcus's work was commanding attention, a stark contrast to the usual praises reserved for the more conventional pieces. Ash watched quietly, his gaze flicking over to Addie's desk.

Her emerald essence seemed to smoke at the corner again. Ash realized that it looked similar to all the times when Miss

Hart complimented his art pieces, but he kept his thoughts to himself.

He quickly shifted his focus back to his own canvas, feeling a tightness in his chest as the lesson continued. He had to respect Miss Hart's words, her advice echoing in his mind: "Unless they ask for help themselves, it's not your business at all."

Ash didn't fully understand what was going on with Addie, but he knew he couldn't force the answers. He couldn't step into her world unless she invited him in. His job, for now, was to be her friend.

Ash sat quietly in his seat, his fingers wrapped around his pencil as he considered his next move. He wanted to say something to Marcus, to acknowledge the strength it had taken to create such a vulnerable piece of art. Yet, he hesitated. He knew how carefully Marcus kept his distance from others. He'd learned that lesson the hard way during their earlier encounter. Offering praise or recognition might only make Marcus feel cornered or exposed.

But there was another reason for his hesitation: Addie. He didn't want to make her feel like she was being overlooked or left out. She was a friend, too, and Ash didn't want to create any tension between them.

When the bell rang, signaling the end of the class, Ash started packing his things, trying not to acknowledge Marcus's feelings too overtly, treating him like any other classmate, but it wasn't easy.

Addie turned to him with a smile, eager for the next part of their routine. "Let's go, Ash. I'm starving, and I want to see what you brought for lunch."

Ash smiled back, relieved to shift gears. "Sure, let's go."

The two of them walked together to the cafeteria, chatting idly, their steps light. As they settled into their usual spot at the table, pulling out their lunches, Ash noticed someone had followed them. He didn't need to look to know who it was.

Marcus sat beside Ash without saying a word, his presence noticeable but not overwhelming. Addie, who was sitting across from Ash, stiffened at the sudden intrusion, clearly uncomfortable with the unexpected change. But Ash simply continued with his routine, trying not to smile as he reached into his bag and pulled out a grilled cheese and tomato sandwich.

He handed one to Addie, keeping one for himself, and then placed the third sandwich between him and Marcus—a silent offering. He didn't force it. He didn't ask. He simply let it be.

For a moment, Marcus didn't move. His aura was still tightly wound, jagged edges of defensive energy clinging to him. But slowly, his hand reached out, taking the sandwich. It felt like a breakthrough. Ash could feel the first signs of Marcus's energy softening, just the smallest crack in the wall he had built around himself.

Ash wanted to smile and show his happiness, but he kept his face neutral, hiding behind his sandwich as he took a bite.

Sitting across from them, Addie glanced from Ash to Marcus and back again. Her discomfort was obvious, but Ash knew it would take time. For now, he shifted the conversation to something lighter.

"So, Addie," he began, his voice casual, "what's that art piece you're working on? I saw some of it earlier in class. It looks great." He paused, watching her closely. "You could really go into animation someday, you know? You'd make a pretty good illustrator."

Addie blinked, startled by his words. "You really think so?"

Ash nodded, his tone genuine as he said, "Yeah, definitely. You've got a talent for bringing things to life."

Addie's face softened, a shy smile tugging at her lips. "Thanks, Ash. I'll think about it."

The conversation settled into a comfortable rhythm as the three of them ate. Marcus, though still quiet, seemed less tense now. There was a strange kind of peace at the table—as if everything, at least for now, was okay with the world.

Chapter 9: Addie's Notebook

Ash ran a hand through his hair, the other tapping his pencil against the library table in a distracted rhythm. After lunch, he, Addie, and Marcus had decided to head to the library to catch up on assignments. With all their other commitments, they didn't often have time to study at home, so the library served as their refuge for getting things done before moving on to the next activity.

Although new to the group, Marcus didn't seem fazed by the pressure, opening his textbooks with a quiet sigh of resignation. Addie, however, offered Ash a small, knowing smile as they all settled into the familiar silence of their study session. The only sounds filling the air were the rustling of pages, the occasional scratch of pen against paper, and the hum of voices echoing faintly across the distant bookshelves.

Minutes passed, comfortable and uninterrupted. It was the kind of quiet Ash appreciated—one where thoughts could flow freely and without distraction. When the bell rang to signal the end of the period, Addie and Marcus began packing up their things, ready to head to their next class, but Ash remained in his chair.

Addie paused mid-motion, her gaze flicking to him, then to Marcus, who raised an eyebrow. Ash met their eyes, offering a half-smile. "It's free period next. I can do whatever."

Marcus gave a nonchalant shrug, slinging his bag over his shoulder. "Cool. Later," he said.

"See you later," Addie added with a small wave.

As they walked away, Ash allowed the silence of the library to settle around him once more. He returned to his work, his pencil moving in a slow, steady rhythm, the words on the page beginning to take shape. But after a while, his concentration began to slip, and his throat felt dry.

He needed a break. So, he stood up, stretching the tightness from his limbs, and made his way over to the water fountain near the entrance. The cold water was a welcome relief, clearing the fog that had settled over his mind. But when he returned to his seat, something on the floor caught his attention.

It was right beneath the chair where Addie had been sitting earlier. Looking closer, Ash realized it was a sketchbook—open, face-down. Without thinking, Ash reached down and carefully picked it up, intending to return it to its owner. His fingers brushed over the worn cover as he flipped it open, searching for a name. But what he found was something completely different from what he expected.

The pages were filled with illustrations that felt eerily alive—figures swirling in an overlay of vibrant lines. Ash's heart skipped a beat as he recognized the familiar sensation depicted in the drawings. These weren't just random sketches; the images mirrored what he saw in people's auras—the swirling, jagged lines of stress, the clouded, muted shades of sadness, and the bright, warm glow of hope.

As Ash continued flipping through the sketchbook, the drawings grew more personal, more revealing—almost too much for him to bear. The first one that made him stop and take a deep breath was of himself. The figure on the page was hunched over in a classroom, shoulders stiff, surrounded by a chaotic swirl of sharp angles and jagged black lines. The rough strokes radiated tension, just like the feeling that gripped his chest when he couldn't block out the noise of a crowded room or when the energy around him became too overwhelming.

"Anxiety clouds," the label beside the drawing read.

Ash's throat tightened. Although he could see the essence in others, he had never glimpsed his own. Yet, if he did have an essence, this was precisely how he envisioned it.

But how? He had never shared his struggles with Addie—not the full extent of them. The overwhelming pressure he sometimes felt, the constant hum of others' emotions buzzing in the back of his mind—it was something he kept locked away. And yet, somehow, Addie had captured it with remarkable ease. She had seen it without knowing what it was, without him ever uttering a word.

He turned the page, his pulse quickening, and there, in quick, decisive strokes, was another sketch of him. This time, he was sitting at his desk, hands gripping the edges, eyes wide, as if trapped in a moment of intense focus.

Surrounding him were swirling, fractal-like patterns, twisting and turning in intricate shapes that seemed to pulse with nervous energy. The lines appeared structured, not chaotic, like an elaborate web of thought. The patterns bled into one another, overlapping and distorting with ease.

"Focus fractals," the phrase next to it read.

Ash's heart skipped a beat. How could she know? How could she understand what it felt like when his mind tried to settle on something—anything—and it felt like his thoughts were caught in a storm of endless spirals? How could she have seen this? It was as if she could peer into the chaos that plagued his mind, the way his thoughts splintered and scattered under pressure.

Addie had seen it; she had seen him. It was as if she had a map of his inner world, one he had never given her access to. How much had she known about him without him saying a single word?

The sharp ring of the bell snapped Ash out of his spiraling thoughts, the sound slicing through the quiet library like a cold breeze. His pulse was still racing as he closed the sketchbook, fumbling slightly with the edges as he tucked it under his arm.

He glanced around, almost expecting someone to catch him in the act, but the library was still mostly empty. Addie's forgotten sketchbook pressed heavily against him, filled with more truth than he was prepared for. His fingers trembled for a moment before he shoved his things into his bag with greater urgency than usual.

Although he knew the sketchbook didn't belong to him, he hesitated to return it. Not before he had the chance to examine it again, to uncover more of what Addie had seen. His hand lingered over the bag before he zipped it up, deliberately adding Addie's sketchbook inside.

With one last glance around the now-empty library, Ash stood up, his legs feeling almost leaden as he made his way to his next class. The hallway seemed distant and muffled as if the world around him had slowed down.

As he walked away, he couldn't help but wonder: What would he discover if he dug deeper into the pages of her sketchbook?

***

Ash stepped through the front door, the familiar scent of home enveloping him. Lily was right behind him, calling out a casual "Hey, Dad!" as they entered. Ash, too, mumbled a quick greeting to his father, who was seated on the couch in the living room, eyes fixed on the TV while he gave him a half-hearted wave.

Without another word, Ash hurried into the kitchen. All he could think about was getting dinner done quickly—he needed to retreat to his room, to the sketchbook, to those images that haunted him. Every chop of the knife, every stir of the pot felt interminable. He wanted to finish and be alone with the sketchbook again so as to understand more of Addie's visions.

Once the table was set, he quickly wiped his hands and fled to his room, barely glancing at Lily and his father, who exchanged a look of quiet surprise at his hasty departure. His father, brows furrowing slightly, asked Lily, "Is he okay?"

Lily, nonchalant as always, shrugged. "Don't know. Let's eat."

Ash closed his bedroom door behind him with a soft click, the familiar quiet enveloping him. He didn't want to dwell on dinner or the tension that might linger in the kitchen. He needed to focus. He needed answers.

His fingers carefully retrieved Addie's sketchbook from his bag, handling it with almost reverent care. The worn edges and soft, fragile pages felt significant in his hands, as though he was holding something deeply personal— something he wasn't entirely meant to see. But the pull was far too strong—he couldn't leave it alone.

Sitting at his desk, he opened it once more. His heart raced as he flipped through more sketches, each more intimate and revealing than the last. Then he came across something that made him pause—a page where the usual sketches gave way to words.

He leaned in, tracing his eyes over the delicate handwriting that filled the page. The words were simple but heavy with meaning:

"I am seen by everyone, yet I am unseen by all."

This time, it wasn't a sketch but a poem, and it struck Ash with unexpected intensity. He could almost feel the words pressing down on him as if they were too close to his own truth.

"I wear a smile like a mask, a persona that fits so well. But underneath, there's a silence, a space where no one dwells."

Ash's fingers hovered over the page as though the words themselves possessed a kind of gravity. He couldn't help but wonder—was this Addie's truth? Did this reflect how she saw herself? The lines spoke of feeling invisible, of hiding behind the version of herself that others expected to see. It mirrored something Ash had always felt deep down—the desire to be understood but the fear of revealing too much, the fear of being seen yet still misunderstood.

Next to the poem was a self-portrait, its lines delicate yet imbued with an odd kind of sadness. Addie's figure was enveloped by swirling grey patterns—subtle, almost like the haze that clouded Ash's perception of her essence. They were the same grey clouds that had occasionally lingered around her emerald essence.

Ash's fingers hovered over the page, almost afraid to touch it. The self-portrait of Addie captured a sorrow he hadn't fully noticed before. Her laughter, always bright, now seemed like a mask, concealing a fragility he had overlooked.

He paused at a page where the word "Invisible" was written in bold strokes. It struck him hard—Addie's vulnerability, hidden behind her confident exterior, mirrored his own. She had managed to capture the essence of what was concealed within, bringing the chaos to light.

Ash's thoughts replayed the changes he had observed in Addie over the past few months. Her art had transformed, much like the darkening of her aura he had sensed. The once vibrant emerald was gradually muting, with greys and blacks creeping in. The brightness he had always associated with her was dimming, supplanted by swirling, sharp patterns that reflected the chaos she had been concealing.

He closed the sketchbook, his fingers lingering on the cover. The decision weighed heavily on him. He hadn't meant to invade her privacy, but the truth was, he didn't know what else to do. The sketches served as a roadmap to understanding how he could help. But at what cost? How much of her was he allowed to see, especially when she had never fully opened up about her own pain?

Ash hesitated. He wasn't sure if keeping the notebook was right, but he couldn't ignore what he had uncovered. Addie was slipping, and if he could use the pages to better understand her needs, perhaps he could help her before it was too late. But he needed to respect her boundaries, too. It felt like a fragile line to walk, one he wasn't sure he could cross without jeopardizing something important between them.

With a deep breath, Ash made his decision. He would keep the notebook for just a while longer. He would use it to understand her better, to figure out how to be there for her without pushing her too far. But he promised himself he would return it to her the moment he felt she was ready.

Ash placed the sketchbook gently on his desk. He wasn't sure what the future held, but for now, he hoped the pages might offer the insight he needed to help Addie—without ever losing sight of the delicate trust between them.

Chapter 10: Vanishing Light

Ash woke the next morning with the sketchbook still clouding in his thoughts, the dark drawings and poetic words lingering in his mind. He had tucked the book away in his bag, having read through most of it before bed. Yet, he still didn't understand everything, and until he did, he wasn't ready to return it. Still, the guilt gnawed at him.

By the time he arrived at school, Ash had already made up his mind—he would avoid Addie, at least for today. He wasn't ready to face her, not with the knowledge of what he had seen in her sketchbook pressing against his chest like a truth waiting to be confessed. If he saw her, it would be too obvious. He wouldn't be able to act normal, and she would sense that something was off.

So, he kept his head down. He moved through the halls quickly, slipping into classrooms before she could spot him. In the library, he chose a corner seat far from where they usually sat together. Even at lunch, he sat with Marcus but kept scanning the cafeteria from the corner of his eye, half-expecting Addie to walk in.

But she never did.

Ash told himself it was a relief—one less thing to worry about. But by the end of the day, an unease had settled deep in his gut. He had assumed they would cross paths eventually—before class, in the hall, somewhere—but the entire school day passed without a single glimpse of her.

Maybe she took the day off. That wasn't too unusual, right?

He told himself not to overthink it, but the next day, it happened again. And then the day after that.

Now, sitting in Miss Hart's art class, Ash found himself staring at Addie's usual seat, her absence feeling heavier than he expected. The chair sat empty, untouched, yet something lingered there—faint traces of dark grey essence still clinging to the space. It made his stomach churn. The essence didn't stay behind like that unless someone had been carrying something heavy, something they couldn't quite let go of.

Ash swallowed hard, gripping his pencil but not moving it across the page. He simply couldn't focus.

Marcus, who was sitting beside him, followed his gaze. "What's up with her?"

Ash shrugged, forcing himself to look away. "Don't know." It wasn't a lie, but it wasn't the full truth either. He hesitated before adding, "I've been trying to text her and all, but she isn't replying."

Marcus raised an eyebrow. "Maybe she's sick."

Ash nodded absently. "Maybe."

But something about it didn't sit right. Addie would have at least sent a quick response—something short, even just to say she wasn't up for talking. Instead, there was silence. And that silence felt louder than anything else.

He turned his gaze back to her empty chair, gripping his pencil a little tighter. He hoped Addie would come back soon. Now, more than anything, he regretted keeping the sketchbook. If he had returned it right away, would things have been different? Would she have still disappeared like this?

He didn't know. But what he did know was that the empty space where Addie should have been was starting to trigger alarm bells in his mind.

As Miss Hart instructed them to begin sketching, Ash seized the chance to open his cell phone, something he rarely did during class. He went straight to his messages, scrolling through the thread where he had been relentlessly sending texts to Addie over the past few days. Still, no reply.

His fingers hesitated over the keyboard as an idea struck him. He rarely used Instagram—his sister, Lily, had set one up for him, but he only posted the occasional art picture. Still, if Addie wasn't responding to messages, maybe she had posted something there.

Opening the app, he quickly searched for her profile, but to no avail—there were no new stories, no recent posts. As he scrolled down, he noticed something unsettling. Before she disappeared three days ago, Addie's posts had begun to change. Her usually bright and lively artwork transitioned into something else—colors fading into muted tones, captions becoming sparse and cryptic.

The shift was gradual but unmistakable. A painting of an open window captioned: "Out there, maybe." A sketch of a faceless figure, simply labeled: "Drifting." A photo of her own hands, smudged with charcoal, the words beneath it reading: "Trying, but I don't know what for."

Ash's grip on his phone tightened. His stomach churned. He wasn't sure he could ignore this any longer. But what could he do? He didn't know Addie's address or her parents' contact information. The one thing he had was her phone number, but even that wasn't working.

Ash exhaled sharply, locking his phone and staring down at his blank sketchbook—the lines he was supposed to be drawing blurred in his mind. Addie was slipping through the cracks, and he had no idea how to reach her.

***

Soon, the class ended, and Ash was left staring blankly at his empty canvas until Marcus snapped him out of it.

"Ash, what's up, dude? You've been pretty out of it."

Ash looked up at Marcus and replied, "I'm good. I'm okay."

It was then that Miss Hart coughed, making sure Marcus and Ash looked at her. She asked Marcus sweetly, "Marcus, would you give us a moment?"

Ash was shocked and didn't know how to stop Miss Hart. Only a week ago, Marcus had an outburst against the math teacher, and Ash didn't want Miss Hart to be at the receiving end of the same outburst. But surprisingly, Marcus nodded and left after telling Ash, "I'll be waiting outside."

Ash nodded as Marcus left, watching the door swing shut behind him. The moment Marcus was out of earshot, Miss Hart turned her attention back to him.

"Everything okay, Ash? You haven't even touched your canvas today. That's unlike you."

Ash swallowed, his fingers tightening around the strap of his bag. "I'm fine, Miss Hart." But the look in her eyes suggested that she didn't quite believe him.

He ran a hand through his hair, staring at the untouched sketchbook in front of him. Then, he admitted in a lower voice this time, "Actually… I'm worried about Addie."

Miss Hart's expression softened. She pulled a chair closer and sat beside him patiently. "Tell me."

Ash hesitated, trying to articulate the turmoil inside him. "I know you've told me before that we can't force people to accept help," he began, "But Addie—she's been absent for days. She won't answer my texts. She hasn't posted anything online. And even before this, she wasn't… okay." He forced himself to meet Miss Hart's gaze. "She's my friend. How am I supposed to just sit here and pretend everything's fine when I know it's not?"

Miss Hart was quiet for a moment, absorbing his words. Then she nodded thoughtfully. "Miss Addie Madison… Yes, I noticed she hasn't been in class for the past three days."

She folded her hands on the desk. "You know, she is the only student who pours her emotions into her work, and lately, those emotions have been dark."

Ash clenched his jaw. He had felt it too—in the sketchbook Addie had left behind, in the way her brushstrokes had turned harsh and erratic as if her feelings were too big to contain.

"Art is a language, Ash," Miss Hart continued. "Sometimes, it's the only way someone knows how to say, 'I'm hurting.' I've seen it before, and I know how helpless it can make you feel. But the truth is…" She sighed. "Unless she lets you in, there's only so much you can do."

Ash's frustration spiked. That was exactly what he didn't want to hear. How could he just accept that? How could he stand by while Addie slipped further away? He was about to argue—about to say that waiting wasn't an option—when Miss Hart raised a hand, stopping him before he could even get the words out.

"But," she added, "you are her friend. And that means you don't have to just wait. You have every right to be concerned. You have every right to check in, to make sure she's okay." She tilted her head slightly. "Have you tried reaching out to her other friends? Or her family?"

Ash hesitated. Addie never really talked about her family, and if she had other close friends, he didn't know them well. That realization hit him hard. How had he never noticed before? How little did he actually know about her world outside of the art room?

"I—" He swallowed. "I don't really know anyone. But I'll try. I have to."

Miss Hart gave him a reassuring nod. "That's all you can do, Ash. And sometimes, that's enough to make a difference."

Ash let out a slow breath and stood up, gathering his things. "Thanks, Miss Hart."

Her smile was warm. "Anytime, child."

Ash nodded before stepping out of the art room, his mind racing with what to do next. He thought he was prepared to face the world—only to be immediately hit by the harsh reality of it.

He had forgotten to put on his glasses and headphones.

The moment he stepped into the hallway, the vibrant and chaotic essence of the students burned through his eyeballs, and the rumbling energy of the crowded space crashed into him like a wave. His stomach lurched, nausea clawing up his throat. His knees buckled, and before he even registered it, he was down. For a brief, awful second, he thought he might actually throw up right there in the middle of the hallway.

Marcus, who had been waiting outside, sighed and crossed his arms. "I really want to ask—why does your face twist like that every time you step out here?" Then he sniffed himself. "I don't smell, do I?"

Ash barely had the energy to wave his hand. "It's not you," he fumbled through his bag. "It's just... my eyes are really light-sensitive, and I can't take the crowd pressure well."

Marcus nodded, surprisingly understanding. "Right. That makes sense."

Ash finally found his glasses, shoving them onto his face before pulling on his hoodie and slipping his headphones over his ears. The world immediately felt a little more bearable, a little less raw. Marcus helped him up, and they started walking toward their next class.

But Ash's mind was elsewhere. His thoughts clashed violently against each other, tangled and restless.

How was he supposed to help Addie when he could barely handle a crowded hallway? He had spent years keeping his head down, avoiding unnecessary interactions, and limiting himself to the few people who made the world tolerable. His ADHD, his sensitivity to essence, the way everything felt too much—none of it was suited for reaching out to people he didn't know.

And yet, what choice did he have?

If he wanted to help Addie, he had to step outside his comfort zone. He had to reach out and find someone—her parents, her friends, anyone who could tell him what was going on. It went against every fiber of his being, but Ash knew he had to act.

He barely noticed how his grip tightened around the strap of his bag, his thoughts tangled in knots. He had made up his mind—he was going to find a way to reach Addie. But the "how" still loomed over him like a wall too tall to climb.

Marcus, who was walking beside him, glanced over. "Still worried about Addie?"

Ash nodded, barely processing the question.

Marcus sighed, then asked, "Want help?"

Ash stopped mid-step, turning to stare at him. "You'll help me?" He hadn't expected Marcus to offer.

Marcus raised an eyebrow. "Why wouldn't I?"

Ash opened his mouth, then closed it again. He didn't have an answer for that. Maybe he just wasn't used to people offering help so freely. After a pause, he admitted, "Yeah… I need help. I want to know if Addie's okay, but I—I don't even know where she lives. I don't have her parents' number. How am I supposed to reach her?"

Marcus smirked as if the answer was obvious. "You just need to think outside the box. Don't worry about it—I'll get you the address."

Ash's stomach twisted. He didn't know if that was reassuring or concerning. "And how exactly are you going to do that? The school doesn't just give out information like that."

Marcus shot him a look, irritated now. "Do you want my help or not?"

Ash hesitated but eventually nodded. "Yeah. Yeah, I do."

Marcus shrugged. "Then leave it to me. I'll send you the details before the last class." Then, as if to make things clear, he added, "But I'm not going with you to her house. I've got something else to do."

Ash frowned, a mix of gratitude and unease settling in his chest. He wasn't sure what Marcus planned to do, and honestly, he wasn't sure he wanted to know. But right now, this was the best shot he had.

"Alright," Ash said finally. "Thanks."

Marcus just waved him off.

***

True to his word, Marcus sent Ash the address before the end of the last class. Ash stared at the message, rereading it as if the numbers and the name of the street would suddenly reveal some hidden meaning. His fingers hovered over his phone, torn between gratitude and a gnawing sense of unease. He scanned the room, searching for Marcus, but he was nowhere to be found.

Ash really hoped he hadn't done anything reckless to get this information. But now wasn't the time to dwell on it. He shoved his phone into his pocket and exhaled. The longer he waited, the harder this would be.

Before heading out, he made a quick stop at Miss Hart's art room. She looked up from her desk, studying him for a moment before simply saying, "Take care, Ash."

That was it—no questions, no lectures, just trust. He nodded and left.

Lily, however, was another story.

She was standing by the gym lockers with her arms crossed and her expression skeptical. "Does Dad know you're going somewhere else?"

Ash hesitated for half a second before nodding. "Of course, he knows."

Lily's eyes narrowed. "Whiteout, I don't know where you're going or what you're planning, but if you're not back home by the time I get back, I'm calling the police."

Ash nearly choked. "What? Why?"

Lily didn't even blink. "Because you never go out of the house unless absolutely necessary. You freak out the second you step into a crowd without your glasses. You act like the world is trying to swallow you whole. And now, suddenly, you're leaving school early? Alone? Yeah, I'm worried."

Ash groaned, rubbing his temples. "Lily, do you even think of me as your big brother? I'm supposed to be the one worrying about you."

Lily smirked. "I do think of you as my big brother. That's why I'm worried."

He sighed. "Come on, Lily. I promise I'll be back soon, and I'll keep in touch, okay?"

Lily stared at him, clearly debating whether to fight him on this. Finally, she let out an exaggerated sigh. "Fine. But if you do anything stupid, I will say, 'I told you so.'"

Ash huffed a small laugh. "Noted."

As he turned toward the exit, his heart pounded against his ribs. His body screamed at him to stay where it was safe, to let this be someone else's problem. But Addie wasn't someone else. She was his friend.

***

Ash took the school bus, gripping the strap of his bag as the city blurred past the window. His foot tapped restlessly against the floor, his thoughts spiraling between anxiety and determination. What if this wasn't really Addie's address? What if Marcus had somehow pranked him? What if her parents slammed the door in his face?

No, Ash told himself. Marcus might be a lot of things, but he wouldn't joke about this.

When the bus finally pulled up near the neighborhood, Ash stepped off and looked around. His breath hitched.

The area was… nice.

Not just nice—high-end. Large houses with pristine driveways, immaculately trimmed hedges, and expensive cars parked out front. He felt out of place immediately.

Ash adjusted his bag and took a deep breath. *It's just a house. A house where Addie lives. That's all.*

But his legs refused to move for a moment.

He had never been great at this—walking up to someone's door, speaking to strangers, putting himself in situations that made his heart race like this.

It's for Addie. Just do it.

Repeating the thought like a mantra, Ash forced himself to move, stepping onto the cobblestone pathway that led up to a two-story home. The garden was beautifully tended, featuring neat rows of flowers and a small stone fountain near the entrance.

The sign beside the door read: *The Madisons.*

Ash swallowed, adjusting his glasses before reaching up to knock.

For a moment, nothing happened. Then, after a few beats, the door cracked open.

A woman stood there, looking exhausted. Dark circles shadowed her eyes, and her blond hair was tied into a loose bun, with a few strands falling out of place. She blinked at him, her brows furrowing slightly.

"Yes? You are?"

Ash hesitated, suddenly hyper-aware of how small his voice felt.

Slowly, he reached up to remove his glasses, then his headphones, and finally his hoodie—exposing himself completely. No barriers, no safety net.

"My name is Ash," he said, slightly unsteady. "I'm Addie's friend from school."

The woman's expression flickered with surprise. She stared at him for a moment before stepping aside and opening the door a little wider.

"Come in."

Ash hesitated.

Was this the right place? Had Marcus actually gotten it right? Or had he just walked into a complete stranger's house?

But I have come this far.

Trusting Marcus—trusting himself—he stepped inside. Suddenly, he was hit by a dense, heavy essence—not suffocating like the black smoke he sometimes sensed around people drowning in their own destruction, but thick with exhaustion, overwhelmingly pressing down from all sides. It was blue, but not the serene blue of the ocean or sky. It was a deep, dragging blue, the color of sleepless nights and silent grief.

He swallowed, adjusting to the feeling as he followed Addie's mother through the house. She moved quietly, like someone who had forgotten how to take up space, her posture slightly slumped despite the elegance of her surroundings.

The living room was pristine, but it felt... untouched. Like it had been cleaned out of habit rather than lived in. A grand bookshelf lined one wall, filled with books that looked more like decorations than items that had been read recently. A single cup sat abandoned on the coffee table, its contents untouched.

"Sit, please," she said softly, disappearing into the kitchen.

Ash hesitated before lowering himself onto the edge of the couch, his fingers curling over the strap of his bag and his knee bouncing anxiously.

A minute later, Addie's mother returned with a glass of water, setting it down in front of him before folding her hands together. There was something distant in her expression, as if she were running through a dozen thoughts at once but wasn't sure which one to settle on.

"I'm sorry, Ash," she said at last. "But Addie isn't home right now."

A prickle of unease crept up Ash's spine, tightening his grip on his bag. "May I ask where she is?"

She hesitated.

That was enough to make his chest tighten further.

Leaning forward slightly, Ash chose his words carefully. "Ma'am… I've been very worried about Addie." Slowly, he reached into his bag and pulled out her sketchbook. "She left this at school the other day." He exhaled. "I found it, and— I'm sorry, but I went through it. I know it's not mine to look through, but I—" He cut himself off, gathering his thoughts before speaking again.

"She always hides behind a smile," he said quietly. "She doesn't talk about what's wrong, but I see it. It's in her art. It's in the way she moves, how her hands shake when she thinks no one's looking, how her smiles don't reach her eyes anymore." His voice grew softer. "She draws beautifully, but her artwork always seems so… sad. It's as if she's carrying the weight of the world, and I don't know how to help her if I don't even know what's wrong."

He set the sketchbook on the table and pushed it toward Addie's mother. "Please," he said. "Can you tell me if she's okay?"

For a long moment, Addie's mother didn't move. She stared at the sketchbook as if it were something fragile, something she wasn't sure she wanted to open.

Then, slowly, she reached for it.

Ash watched as she turned the pages, her fingers trembling slightly as she took in each piece. His stomach twisted at the way her lips parted in quiet shock, the way her expression crumbled as she traced over a poem Addie had written in the margins.

A sob escaped her throat, and she lifted a hand to her mouth, pressing her fingers against her lips as her shoulders shook.

Ash sat still, his heart pounding, unsure if he had made things worse.

Finally, in a voice that was barely more than a whisper, Addie's mother said, "Addie had to be admitted to a mental health facility."

The words settled over Ash like a thick fog, numbing at first, before their weight sank deep into his chest.

He blinked, his thoughts stuttering, trying to grasp something—anything—that would make this feel less like reality.

"A facility?" His voice came out small.

"She…" Addie's mother swallowed, her fingers tightening around the sketchbook. "She wasn't doing well. We didn't realize how bad it had gotten. She didn't tell us. She just kept pretending everything was fine until—" Her voice broke, and she exhaled shakily before composing herself. "Until it wasn't."

Ash felt something inside him crack. His hands curled into fists on his lap. He had known Addie wasn't okay. He had felt it, seen it in the way her aura dimmed, in how the edges of her presence frayed like an unraveling thread. And still, he hadn't done enough.

If he had spoken up sooner—if he had pushed instead of waiting, instead of assuming she would be okay—would she still be here?

His gift flickered violently, his senses blurring. For a brief, dizzying moment, the room around him felt stretched and distorted, like he wasn't fully there. Addie's mother's essence pulsed erratically, thick with exhaustion, sorrow, and something deeper—guilt, perhaps, mirroring his own.

Ash forced himself to take a breath, grounding himself before he got lost in it.

"Can I see her?" he asked, his voice almost hesitant, like he wasn't sure if he deserved to.

Addie's mother studied him for a long moment. Then, softer this time, she said, "I'll have to check with the facility first."

Ash nodded, unable to find words.

As he sat there, staring at the sketchbook Addie had left behind, one thought looped over and over in his mind.

"I—" he hesitated, "If there's anything else I can do. Anything she needs. Just… let me know."

Addie's mother gave him a tired but grateful nod. "I'll let her know."

Ash swallowed against the lump in his throat and pushed himself to stand. He left behind a "Thank you" because the silence felt a bit too much.

As he stepped outside, the cold air hit him like a wall. It seeped through his hoodie, into his bones, until he wasn't sure if he was shivering from the chill or something else. His fingers curled and uncurled at his sides.

His world had become so quiet that his thoughts sounded loud—too loud. He took a breath, then another, but it wasn't enough to push down the tightness coiling in his stomach.

She'd be okay. She has to be.

But that thought didn't settle the way he wanted it to. It didn't stop the weight pressing against his ribs, the nausea crawling up his throat, the exhaustion pulling at his limbs.

Ash exhaled shakily and started walking, hands stuffed into his pockets, head down.

The cold stayed with him, lingering under his skin.

Chapter 11: The Loss

After leaving the Madisons' house, Ash waited at the bus stop for longer than half an hour. The cold had crept into his fingers, and exhaustion settled on his shoulders, but Ash didn't feel it. By the time he finally found a bus heading home, the sky had already darkened, and the streets were swallowed in dim pools of streetlight. He arrived just as Lily and his father, John, were about to make a call to the authorities.

The tension in the air was palpable the second he stepped through the door.

"Where have you been?" John asked, worried, though he tried to keep his voice even. "You should've been home ages ago."

Lily stood beside him, arms crossed. "We were about to call the cops, Ash. You weren't answering your phone."

Ash only shrugged as he kicked off his shoes. "It just took some time to find a bus heading home."

He didn't offer anything more than that—no explanations, no reassurances, just that single, detached statement before he walked into the kitchen and started making dinner. He continued with the same old routine as if he hadn't just been missing for a long time.

Lily and John exchanged glances—something felt off. It was as if Ash was trying to maintain a distance between them, and neither of them knew how to approach him. By the time they decided to speak again, Ash was already gone—back in his room with the door locked behind him.

The moment he shut the door, he threw himself onto his bed, burying his face in the pillow. His hands clenched into fists at his sides, nails biting into his palms. A slow, simmering anger churned inside him—not toward anyone else, but at himself.

He knew Addie wasn't doing well, and what had he done about it? Nothing. If he couldn't use his ability to help those he cared about, what on earth was it good for?

The thought spiraled over and over, tangling in his mind like a knot that refused to come undone. He lay there, unmoving, eyes shut in a futile attempt to will himself into sleep. Maybe if he was lucky, the exhaustion would take over, and he wouldn't have to feel this way. But sleep continued to elude him.

Hours passed, and his room sank into silence until, at some point, there was a knock on his door—followed first by Lily's voice, then his father's. He neither moved nor did he answer. Then, he heard his father sigh and heard him say, "Maybe he's fallen asleep. Let's go. We'll check on him in the morning."

Ash still lay there, eyes closed, hearing their footsteps fade away. His body ached with the weight of his own thoughts, the frustration sitting like a stone in his chest. And even as the hours dragged on and night turned into morning, he remained restless.

When his alarm finally rang, Ash forced his eyes open. His body felt leaden, his mind thick with exhaustion. He exhaled slowly, staring at the ceiling. He was supposed to get up, get moving, and follow the same routine as always. But for the first time in a long while, he didn't know if he had the energy to pretend.

Pushing himself upright, he blinked against the heaviness in his head. His vision blurred, the world around him smudging together. He rubbed his eyes, waiting for the fog to lift, but it didn't.

Panic crept up his spine. Why couldn't he see clearly? His breathing hitched as his fingers clutched the edge of his blanket. Was something wrong? Was he—?

Then, slowly, the haze dissipated. He let out a shaky breath, relief flooding through him. Maybe it was just exhaustion, or maybe he had gotten up too fast. Either way, he didn't have time to dwell on it. He got up, went to freshen up, brushed his teeth, and prepared for school. After taking his meds, he stepped out of his room, knocking on Lily's door on his way to the kitchen.

As he started breakfast, Lily's voice rang out behind him. "You're up early."

"I slept early," he said, turning to glance at her—only to feel his stomach drop.

Her comforting blue essence was nowhere to be seen.

His breath caught as he immediately shut off the stove. "Lily," he said, his voice sharper than intended. He hurried toward her, scanning her up and down. "Are you okay?"

Lily blinked, confused. "Yeah? Why wouldn't I be?"

She wasn't lying—Ash knew that much from her expression, from the way she looked at him with clear, open eyes. Then why? Why couldn't he see it?

The morning's blurry vision flashed through his mind. His heart pounded as realization crawled over his skin. If he couldn't see Lily's essence, something must be wrong with her. And if it wasn't her, then—

Something was wrong with him.

His thoughts spiraled, twisting faster than he could control. His breath turned shallow, chest tightening as his surroundings dimmed. He could barely hear Lily's voice calling his name. Could barely register her hands on his shoulders.

"Dad!" Lily's voice was shaking. "Dad, something's wrong with Ash!"

His father was there in an instant. "Ash, breathe," he instructed, voice steady but firm. "In and out, son. Follow me."

Ash clung to the sound, forcing himself to follow his father's lead. Slowly, painfully, the world steadied, though the unease remained lodged in his bones.

His father studied him with concern. "Did you take your meds?"

Ash nodded weakly. "Yeah, I took them."

His father's frown deepened. "Maybe we should visit the hospital."

"No," Ash said quickly, shaking his head. "It's fine, Dad. It was just a small panic attack. I'm sure it was nothing."

He didn't want to worry him. He still remembered the time his father didn't come home—how everything had crumbled around them. He couldn't let that happen again.

Lily and their father exchanged a look, still unsettled. "Are you sure?" Lily asked.

"I'm sure." Ash forced a nod. "And we need to go to school. It's getting late."

Neither of them looked convinced, but they didn't push further. Ash turned back to finish breakfast, but his hands were still shaking.

Something was wrong. He couldn't see his father's essence as well. Something like the colors—his gift—dimming had happened for the first time. It felt like he was losing signal to a frequency he never thought could fade.

As soon as they headed out, Ash pulled on his hoodie, tugging the sleeves over his hands as if the fabric could shield him from the unease curling in his stomach. He slid on his headphones, though he wasn't playing anything yet, and adjusted his glasses on the bridge of his nose. Even if he couldn't see the essences, he at least wanted to maintain some sort of normalcy.

He didn't know what was happening with the essences.

Was it a good thing? Maybe. He wanted to think it was a good riddance. No more overwhelming emotions bleeding into his senses, no more suffocating colors twisting around him, no more annoying buzz. But the absence of it—the quiet, empty space where it should have been—made his chest feel hollow.

It wasn't just some ability he had. It had become a part of him, something he had learned to navigate, something that had, in its own strange way, helped him hold on to the fragile pieces of his family.

And Ash feared losing that again.

Still, he swallowed his unease and forced himself to act normal. He couldn't let it get to him—not now.

Lily, however, wasn't buying it.

She kept one eye on him the entire way to school, her usual chatter less energetic than normal, like she was watching for any signs that he might crack again.

When they got off the bus, Ash expected her to split off toward her group of friends like she always did, but she didn't.

He frowned, turning to her. "Why aren't you going?"

Her friends were right there, waiting at the entrance, but Lily just crossed her arms. "So what? I want to hang out with my brother today."

Ash's stomach sank. This was definitely because of his panic attack that morning. He sighed. "I really am fine, Lily."

"What? Are you seriously telling me, your own sister, to go away?" Lily scoffed.

Ash hesitated. He wasn't sure what to say. He wanted her to go, to be with her friends, to not worry about him, but before he could say anything, she shrugged.

"I don't feel like going with them today," she said. "Their conversations are getting old, you know? It's always about boys now." She made a face. "Why? We're still twelve!"

Ash blinked, caught off guard. He had no idea how to respond to that. He didn't want Lily worrying about him, but also... why were twelve-year-olds talking about boys already? Why? They didn't have to!

So, instead of arguing, he let her tag along as he went to his locker, grabbing his books for class. He figured he'd walk her to her classroom afterward, but when they reached his own class first, Lily stopped.

"This is your class, right? Go in."

Ash hesitated. Was she... dropping him off?

Heat crept up his face. That was supposed to be his job—not the other way around.

Feeling slightly embarrassed, he gave a small nod and turned toward the door. Before stepping inside, he glanced back at Lily, who just grinned knowingly.

Shaking his head, he walked in, but no matter where he went, he couldn't ignore it. Something that had followed him for more than half his life was now gone, and its absence pressed against him like a weight.

At first, he tried to convince himself that it was nothing. Maybe he was just exhausted. Maybe it would come back. But as he walked through the halls, past rows of students chatting, laughing, and arguing, his stomach twisted.

He had always seen the colors, even with his glasses on, even if they were dull. A flicker here, a muted glow there— just enough to remind him of what lay beneath the surface of people's words. But now, even when he slipped his glasses off, squinting at the faces around him, there was nothing— no shimmering lights curling around their silhouettes, no soft pulses of emotions woven into their movements. There was just… silence.

He swallowed hard, pushing forward.

Keep moving. Act normal.

His fingers trembled as he grabbed his books from his locker. He clenched his jaw and flexed his hands to keep them steady. Maybe if he just focused on the routine, it wouldn't get to him. He would go to class, take notes, and move through the day like always.

But the silence was suffocating.

Without the essences, the world felt eerily dull, as if someone had sucked all the life out of it. It should've been liberating. He had always hated how overwhelming the colors could be—how they crashed into him without warning, how they made everything *too much*. But now, without them, the world felt distant and unfamiliar, like he was walking through a foggy dream where nothing quite belonged to him.

He dug his fingers into the sleeves of his hoodie as he entered the classroom. The lesson droned on, but he wasn't processing a single word. His mind was a tangled mess of questions. Was this permanent? Had he done something wrong?

Was something broken inside him? And, worst of all—if the essences were gone, did that mean something was missing in him too?

A sharp, nervous tremor ran through his hands. He balled them into fists beneath the desk, pressing them against his thighs to steady himself. He just needed to get through the day—that was all. Just a few more hours, and then he could lock himself in his room and figure this out. But the tension in his chest refused to fade.

At some point, time slipped from his grasp. The noise of the classroom dulled into a distant murmur. The walls seemed too close, the air too thin. His vision blurred at the edges, the world tilting slightly. His breaths came short and shallow, but he didn't register it fully—not until someone called his name.

"Hey. Ash, right?"

The voice cut through the haze.

Ash blinked, his surroundings snapping into focus. He turned to see the person sitting next to him staring at him with mild concern.

"Are you okay?"

Ash's gaze flickered to the front of the room. The teacher was gone. The other students were packing up, some already filing out the door.

Class was over?

His stomach twisted.

Without a word, he shoved his books into his bag, slung it over his shoulder, and bolted for the door. He didn't see the way his classmate raised an eyebrow and muttered, "What a weirdo."

He didn't care.

He needed *out*.

He didn't know where he was running. Everything passed in a blur—the halls, the classrooms, the people. His breath came in sharp gasps, his legs moving without direction, without control. He wasn't even sure how he was avoiding crashing into anything—until suddenly, he didn't.

His shoulder clipped someone hard, throwing him off balance. His foot caught on something, and suddenly, the ground was rushing up to meet him. He barely had time to throw out his hands before he hit the floor, the impact jarring through his arms. A bag went flying, sending books and papers scattering across the hallway.

A sharp exhale came from above him.

"You *doofus*!"

Blinking through the haze, Ash barely made out the familiar faces.

And then, everything came crashing down.

Because the person he had run into—the one now towering over him with a murderous glare—was Jackson Chen.

Ash barely had time to process the situation before Jackson grabbed the front of his hoodie, yanking him up as if he weighed nothing. His feet barely touched the ground, his already unsteady vision swimming.

"You worthless little—" Jackson's voice was a low growl, pure irritation flickering in his dark eyes.

Ash didn't fight back. He wasn't sure he *could* fight back. His thoughts were still scrambled, his body weak from the panic attack clawing at his chest.

Then, before the first punch could land, a hand shot out, catching Jackson's wrist mid-air.

"Put him down, Chen," a calm but sharp voice cut through the tension.

It was Marcus.

There was an eerie stillness as the two locked eyes.

"You don't want me to ruin that face, would you?" Marcus added, his grip on Jackson's wrist tightening slightly, just enough to send a warning.

For a second, Jackson hesitated. A flicker of unease passed through his expression before he scoffed and shoved Ash away, letting him stumble back.

"Look after your pug, Marcus," Jackson muttered before walking off, throwing one last glare over his shoulder.

Marcus sighed, running a hand through his hair before crouching down. "Ash? Are you okay?"

Ash didn't answer. He didn't even look at Marcus. His ears were ringing again, his breath shallow, his fingers twitching at his sides. He needed to get away.

Without a word, he turned and walked straight into the nearest room—the art classroom. He shut the door behind him, twisting the lock before Marcus could follow.

"Hey!" Marcus knocked almost immediately. "Ash? Open the door."

Ash pressed his back against the cool surface, his heart still hammering against his ribs. His hands clenched into fists, his whole body trembling. He couldn't handle this—not here, not now.

"Come on, man. Talk to me," Marcus called again.

The knocking was too loud; the world was too loud.

Ash exhaled shakily, scanning the room until his gaze landed on the art supply closet—small, enclosed, and separate.

His feet moved before he could think. He pulled open the door, stepped inside, and sank to the floor, burying his head between his knees. In the muffled darkness, he forced himself to breathe.

In. Out. In. Out.

He counted each breath, willing his racing mind to slow.

Outside, everything was descending into chaos. Marcus was still knocking. More voices joined—murmurs of confusion, whispers spreading among students who had seen Ash rush inside and lock himself in.

Then, a voice cut through the noise.

"What's going on?"

Miss Hart.

Marcus exhaled in visible relief. "Miss—Ash is in there. He locked the door, and I don't know what happened, but he didn't look good."

There was a pause. Then, the distinct jingle of keys. The lock clicked, and Miss Hart and Marcus stepped into the classroom, their eyes scanning the space.

Their hearts lurched—it was empty.

For a brief, horrible second, panic tightened Marcus's throat. *Where had Ash gone?*

Then Miss Hart's gaze flickered to the slightly ajar supply closet.

Gently, she stepped forward and pulled the door open.

And there, curled up on the floor, was Ash.

His hoodie was bunched around his fists, his knees drawn to his chest. His breath was slow but uneven, as if he was barely holding himself together.

Miss Hart crouched in front of him, moving carefully, like approaching a wounded animal. She didn't speak right away. She didn't try to pull him out or demand an explanation. She just sat there.

For a moment, there was only silence. The kind that didn't need filling. Even without the usual kaleidoscope of color that surrounded her, even without the gentle glow that always made her presence known, Miss Hart still felt safe.

And somehow, despite the overwhelming chaos of the past hour, despite the tightness in his chest that still hadn't completely gone away, tears filled Ash's eyes and slipped down his cheeks. He didn't want anyone to see them. He never did. But in front of Miss Hart, he let go. There was no judgment in her gaze, no pressure to pull himself together. With her, he could just exist.

Miss Hart borrowed Marcus's jacket and whispered to him, "Tell the people outside to make space. Don't let anyone come close."

Marcus nodded and went outside, clearing the hallway while Miss Hart gently covered ash within Marcus's jacket. Then, she carefully guided him to the nurse's room, ensuring no one else was allowed inside. Ash was clearly not comfortable with people around.

Every sound—whether a whisper, a conversation, or a distant shout—felt like too much. It pressed in on him, clawing at his skin, making his head throb. He lay down, eyes squeezed shut, trying to block out the world.

Miss Hart gave him space, stepping outside, where Marcus was waiting, "Is he okay?"

"He's okay," Miss Hart assured him. "But he's sensitive to sound, so try not to talk."

That was when John and Lily arrived. Their footsteps were hurried, their voices tight with worry.

"Miss Hart?" John asked, breathless. "Where's my son?"

Lily turned to Marcus, eyes wide. "What happened to Ash?"

Miss Hart held up a hand, gesturing for them to lower their voices. She led them a little farther from the door—just enough so the thin walls wouldn't let the sound seep through.

"Mr. Winters, Lily, please calm down," she said, trying to placate them. "Ash is hypersensitive to sound right now, and he isn't feeling well. I suggest not talking to him for now." She hesitated, then added, "And I really think you should take him to a specialist. It's surprising he's managed this long with such extreme sensitivity to light and sound without any external help."

John frowned. "But he has his meds. As long as he takes them, this shouldn't happen."

Miss Hart's brows knit together. "Meds?"

John hesitated before answering. "He takes them for his ADHD."

Miss Hart's expression shifted. "And… he took them this morning?"

"Yeah," John said. "I asked him, and he said yes."

Miss Hart exhaled, her concern deepening. "Even so, you should still take him to a specialist. I'm not a doctor, and if the medication isn't helping, only a doctor can figure out why."

They all fell silent, lost in their own thoughts. The weight of everything settled between them—concern, guilt, uncertainty until Miss Hart broke the quiet.

"Let's give him some time," she suggested. "When he falls asleep, take him home and let him rest for a few days. He needs a break."

John nodded. "Okay."

Lily stood a little apart, her eyes fixed on the nurse's room door. She hadn't said much, but the tension in her posture spoke volumes. She wanted to see Ash to ensure her brother was okay, but she also didn't want to worsen things.

Marcus, standing beside her, had gone unusually quiet, too. The fact that Ash had ADHD hit him harder than he expected. Marcus had never thought much about it before, but now, he wondered. The way he had glasses and headphones on—like he was shielding himself from the world—suddenly made sense.

And for the first time, Marcus found himself wondering if he had something like that, too.

***

When Ash opened his eyes, he slowly realized he was staring at the ceiling of his bedroom. His head ached, his thoughts felt sluggish, and for a brief, disorienting moment, he wasn't sure how he got here. Did his father bring him home?

He tried to piece together the last thing he remembered, but his mind felt scrambled, as if someone had shaken up all his thoughts and left them in a tangled mess.

Turning his head, he noticed Lily curled up beside him. She was fast asleep, but as he looked closer, he noticed faint streaks on her face—tears that had long since dried. Ash frowned. Had he scared her? What had even happened?

Sometimes, his head got so complicated that he couldn't keep up with it. He sat up carefully, wincing as a sharp headache pulsed behind his eyes. He needed water. Something cold. Maybe if he splashed his face, his brain would clear up.

Dragging himself to his feet, he made his way to the bathroom. The dim glow of the nightlight cast long shadows across the floor as he turned on the faucet. Cold water pooled in his hands, and he lingered for a moment, watching it slip through his fingers before bringing them up to his face. But just as he was about to splash the water on his skin, something made him stop.

His gaze lifted.

The mirror.

He stared at his reflection—and then stared harder. He had always wondered what his own essence was, but he had never seen it. But now there it was—cloudy darkness—a vast, empty void where there usually was none.

Ash's breath hitched. His fingers trembled as he reached out, pressing his fingertips against the glass, half expecting the image to ripple, to change, to show something else. But it didn't.

His chest tightened. *What... what was this?*

The question lodged itself deep inside him, something he wasn't sure he was ready to carry.

Chapter 12: Echoes

Ash continued to look into the void in the mirror, the darkness slowly circling around him like a snake coiling around its prey, its tendrils creeping up his arms and encircling his frame. A faint tinge of purple clung to its edges, a fleeting trace slowly being consumed by a deep, smoky hue. The mist swelled, stretching wider until it was on the verge of completely engulfing him.

The terror was so overwhelming that a choked scream tore from Ash's throat, throwing him backward. His shoulder collided hard against the bathroom tiles on the far wall, but he still turned his eyes away from the mirror. His hands flew to his ears, pressing down as if he could drown it all out.

Tears escaped his clenched eyelids. Nothing made sense. Nothing at all.

Then, the door burst open.

"Ash!"

He heard Lily's voice, followed by his father's, and an alarm was evident in both. There was a rush of movement, and they were beside him in an instant, their hands on his shoulders. Their frantic words blurred at the edges, barely reaching him.

"Ash, talk to me! What happened?"

His father's voice was strong and urgent.

"Hey, hey, breathe, okay?" Lily's touch was gentle but grounding. "You're okay. You're okay."

But he wasn't. He wasn't okay. He didn't know if he would ever be okay again.

And then—

"Ash…"

A voice.

Soft. Familiar. One he rarely heard anymore.

He lifted his head to see his mother standing in the doorway.

She looked pale, thinner than he remembered, but in this moment, none of that mattered. There was something in her eyes—raw, open concern, a kind of softness she hadn't shown in so long.

"My child…" she whispered, stepping forward. "What happened?"

Ash barely registered moving. One moment, he was frozen in place, and the next, he was in her arms, gripping her tightly as if afraid she'd disappear, as if he could anchor himself back to reality just by holding on.

And she let him.

She held him while Ash sobbed into her shoulder, clutching the fabric of her sleeves, shaking, unraveling. And she didn't pull away, nor did she let go.

For the first time in a long while, he allowed himself to cry.

***

Debra held Ash until his sobs quieted, his body growing heavier against her. She didn't move, didn't speak—just let him stay there, safe in her embrace, until exhaustion finally pulled him under.

Carefully, she moved him to his room and eased him onto his bed, tucking the blanket around him. For a long moment, she simply watched him, her expression unreadable. She had always known Ash struggled with his ADHD, but she had never seen him like this—so lost and fragile. And she hadn't been there for him.

A lump rose in her throat as she stepped back, closing the door behind her.

Outside, John and Lily were waiting.

Debra hesitated. It had been a long time since she had ventured out of her room and faced them like this. The air between them felt awkward, thick with unspoken words. But right now, all she cared about was Ash.

"What happened with him?" she forced herself to ask.

Even as the words left her mouth, guilt curled in her chest. She should have known. She was his mother. It was her responsibility to know. But she pushed the self-recrimination aside—Ash needed her, and she couldn't afford to retreat now.

John shifted uncomfortably. Their last fight still lingered between them, raw and unresolved. He wasn't ready to forgive her, not yet. But seeing Ash break down in his mother's arms had reminded him of something undeniable—no matter how much their children tried to act strong, they still needed their mother. They always would.

With a sigh, he turned to Lily. "Go to your room, kiddo."

Lily frowned but didn't argue. She gave their mother a brief glance before retreating down the hall.

John motioned for Debra to follow him—not to their bedroom, but to the living room, a space Debra hadn't allowed herself to occupy until just recently. He wanted to talk to her somewhere she wouldn't be pulled back into her thoughts.

"Let's talk here."

Debra nodded and sat across from him, her hands tightly folded in her lap.

"I think we need to take Ash to a specialist," John said, his voice careful.

She frowned. "Okay. But… why? Did something happen?"

John hesitated. He knew Debra was just as fragile as Ash, and the last thing he wanted was for her to shut down again. He chose his words deliberately.

"Yeah. Something happened. I don't know what exactly, but… his meds aren't working. Or they're not enough. He needs help."

Debra exhaled slowly, absorbing that. "Oh."

Then, after a pause, she murmured, "Call it a mother's instinct, or don't—I haven't been much of a mother, really—but I think you should talk to him."

John studied her, surprised.

"I want to," she admitted, "but I don't know if I'll be able to help. You're the better parent between us." Her voice was quiet, almost self-deprecating. "And… maybe a man could understand a man better." She met his eyes hesitantly. "Is that okay?"

John's initial instinct was to push back, to remind her that being a parent wasn't about gender. But then he looked at her—really looked at her—and saw what this was: an effort, a step forward.

For the first time in years, Debra was present and clear-headed.

He nodded. "Yeah. I can try."

She exhaled in relief and offered him a small, tired smile. "Good."

For the first time in a long while, it felt like they were standing on the same ground—not as husband and wife, not as two people weighed down by resentment, but as parents, trying to do better in their own ways.

***

Ash stirred awake, his gaze drifting to the clock on the nightstand. A faint gray light seeped through the curtains—

the hesitant glow of early morning. The house was quiet, wrapped in the heavy stillness that came before the day truly began. He lay still for a moment, his mind sluggishly catching up with reality.

The last thing he remembered was being in his mother's arms. The memory sent a flush of embarrassment creeping up his neck. He hadn't cried like that in a long time, especially not in front of her. Yet, some part of him still felt the lingering warmth of that moment, as if something inside him had shifted.

But beyond the quiet shame, there was something else he recalled. He shivered as he thought of that thing in the mirror.

The way the darkness had curled around him, thick, stretching until it was suffocating. How it had stretched and twisted, swallowing everything. Never before had he been able to see his own essence. But that thing in the mirror? It was definitely his. A deep, smoky grey, nearly black, with the faintest tinge of purple at the edges—just a whisper of color, as if something still lingered beneath the void.

But how? He hadn't even been able to see others or his mother's dark essence anymore.

He needed answers.

His fingers curled into the sheets as his decision solidified. He would talk to Miss Hart; if anyone knew anything about this, it would be her.

With that settled, Ash pushed himself up, his stomach twisting in protest. He hadn't eaten since... what? Yesterday's lunch? No, even that felt distant. Hunger gnawed at him with full force. He could only hope his family hadn't starved themselves just because he hadn't made dinner.

As he padded toward the door, he passed the bathroom. His steps slowed involuntarily, eyes flickering toward the mirror.

A chill ran down his spine.

He didn't look. He didn't dare. Instead, he hurried past, shaking off the unease.

The house was silent—more silent than usual. That was the first thing he noticed as he made his way downstairs. The TV wasn't on—not even as background noise. His home was always quiet, but this was different.

When he stepped into the kitchen, he halted.

His mother was there.

Debra sat at the table, her head resting on her folded arms. She looked... small, almost as if exhaustion had seeped into her bones.

At the sound of his footsteps, her eyes fluttered open. She yawned, stretching slightly before blinking up at him.

"Oh, Ash," she murmured, rubbing her eyes. "You're awake."

She stood up, smoothing down her sleeves as if trying to shake off the haze. Then, without hesitation, she turned toward the stove.

"You must be hungry," she said, switching on the burner. "Let me heat up the tomato soup for you."

Ash was caught off guard by her presence in the kitchen. But he let it go, thinking she probably felt well enough to come down. He pulled out a chair and sat, watching her. "Tomato soup? For breakfast? Why?"

Debra turned briefly, pressing a hand to his forehead. Her touch was cold and felt soothing against his heated skin.

"You had a fever earlier," she said simply. "It's cooled down now."

Ash blinked, surprised that he hadn't even realized.

"Did Dad and Lily eat last night?" he asked as she set a bowl in front of him.

Debra offered a small, tired smile. "Yes. Both Lily and Dad had their dinner." She hesitated for a moment before her voice softened. "Also, your dad… he's awake and waiting for you in the workshop. Go see him after you eat."

That made Ash pause mid-reach for his spoon.

Waiting for him?

Confused, he glanced up, but Debra had already turned away, busying herself at the sink. He considered asking more, but something in her posture told him not to press. Instead, he picked up his spoon and took a bite.

Warmth flooded his senses, rich and familiar. His mother's cooking. He hadn't realized how much he had missed it. It felt as if it had been forever.

Ash swallowed the last spoonful of soup, letting the warmth settle in his chest. He pushed the bowl away and stood, stretching out his limbs before heading toward the back door.

His mother's gaze lingered on him. He felt it pressing gently against his back, as if she wanted to say something but was holding herself back. He hesitated, glancing over his shoulder. She offered him a small smile before turning back to the sink.

Without a word, he stepped outside. The morning air was crisp, carrying the faint scent of damp grass. A low wind stirred the trees, their branches shifting against the clear blue sky. The workshop stood at the far end of the backyard, the single light inside casting a faint glow through the window.

Ash shoved his hands into his pockets and walked toward it, the gravel crunching softly beneath his feet. He wasn't sure what to expect, but a quiet curiosity stirred within him. His father had never waited for him before.

The door creaked as he pushed it open. Inside, John was hunched over the workbench, his broad shoulders curved forward, concentration evident in the way his hands moved. Ash hesitated in the doorway, glancing around at the scattered tools and wood shavings. The scent of sawdust filled the air, mingling with the faint smell of old varnish.

"Dad?"

John turned slightly, his face illuminated by the overhead light. "Ash, come here."

Ash stepped forward, his eyes flickering to the object his father had been working on. It was a small wooden structure, delicate yet sturdy, with intricate details carved along the edges.

"What is this?" Ash asked, tilting his head.

John smiled, brushing sawdust from his hands. "It's a birdhouse."

Ash blinked. "A birdhouse?"

John nodded, running a hand over the smooth wooden surface. "Yeah. I used to make these all the time when I was a kid. I'd build little houses like this and put them up around the neighborhood. Eventually, birds would start nesting in them, and I'd watch them grow—from hatchlings to adults."

A low chuckle escaped him. "Oh, the neighbors used to be so mad at me. You have no idea."

Ash raised a brow. "Why?"

John leaned back against the workbench, a smirk playing on his lips. "Because I put them everywhere. Trees, fences, even a lamppost once. The whole neighborhood turned into a bird sanctuary. There were nests everywhere—little beaks peeking out, chirping at sunrise." He laughed, shaking his head at the memory. "Old Mr. Thompson nearly had a heart attack when a nest fell onto his front porch. He thought he was being invaded."

Ash found himself smiling—actually smiling. It was rare to hear his father talk about his childhood like this, let alone with such fondness.

John glanced at him, his expression turning thoughtful. "I figured... maybe you'd want to help me finish this one."

Ash hesitated. His father wanted to do something with him? For a moment, he didn't know what to say. But then he stepped closer, fingers grazing the smooth wood.

"Yeah," Ash said finally. "I'd like that."

As Ash and his father worked, he noticed details he'd once overlooked—the slight hesitation in his father's hands, the tension in his shoulders. Without the essence to guide him, he relied on small cues: a shift in stance, a quiet sigh.

He had always seen emotions as color, but now he saw effort—the way his parents pushed through, even when things didn't turn out right. But now, he could see something else too. Right now, they weren't just holding it together for themselves. They were working through their own struggles—for him. And for some reason, that felt good.

***

By the time they finished, the sun had fully risen, casting bright light across the yard. Ash wiped his hands on his jeans, glancing toward the house. If he wanted to make it to school on time, he needed to hurry. Both John and Debra had told him he didn't have to go—said he could take more time if he needed it—but he had to meet Miss Hart regardless. Staying home wouldn't change that.

Lily sat beside him on the bus, watching him with an expression he was starting to get used to. Concern edged with that stubborn protectiveness of hers. She didn't say anything at first, but when the bus slowed near their stop, she shifted forward, ready to follow him.

Ash shook his head. "Lily, I promise I'm okay. I have my meds, my glasses, and my headphones, so I'll be fine."

She hesitated, clearly not convinced.

Then, a familiar voice cut in from behind them. "It's fine. I'll be with him—you should go to class."

Ash blinked as an arm slung over his shoulder. It was Marcus.

Lily exhaled, relief washing over her face as she stepped back. "Good. If anything happens, please call me." She shot Ash a knowing look. "Heaven knows he never would."

Marcus grinned. "Sure thing."

As Lily left, Ash turned toward Marcus, frowning. "What's going on?"

Marcus feigned ignorance. "What's going on?" He shook his head. "Nothing that I know of—except that we might be late to class if we don't move now."

Before Ash could respond, Marcus grabbed his sleeve and pulled him along. The contact made Ash a little uncomfortable—not because he minded Marcus being there, but because fragments of the other day were starting to resurface: the full-blown panic, the loss of control, the crushing weight of everything at once. And Marcus. He remembered Marcus trying to help, standing there while Ash had all but locked him out.

Ash swallowed. "Marcus, thanks for yesterday."

Marcus looked surprised at first, then smiled. "Why are you thanking me? I didn't do anything."

Ash shook his head. "Yeah, but you were there. And you tried. Thanks."

Marcus nodded as if considering it. "You still don't have to thank me. You helped me, so I helped you."

Ash frowned, confused. "When did I help you?"

Marcus grinned. "You did."

Ash narrowed his eyes, trying to recall any specifics, but Marcus didn't elaborate. Instead, he walked beside him, hands in his pockets, as if the argument was already settled.

In the first place, it wasn't like Marcus to force a deeper explanation. He wasn't one to pry or demand things Ash wasn't ready to give. Maybe that's why it felt so easy being around him.

***

The whole day passed without incident, and finally, after the last class, Marcus dropped Ash off at Miss Hart's room.

As soon as he stepped inside, Miss Hart looked up and smiled, "Ash."

Ash did not hesitate. "Miss Hart, there's something I want to tell you."

Her brows lifted slightly in surprise, but she didn't question it. Instead, she pulled another chair across from hers, sat down, and gestured for him to do the same.

Even without the kaleidoscope of colors he once saw around her, Miss Hart still felt warm—like sunlight filtering through leaves. Something about her made it easy to talk.

Ash took a breath. "Miss Hart. I have rarely told anyone this, but I don't know when it started, but I've been able to see people's emotions."

She nodded, unsurprised. "Yes, I know. It's part of why I started tutoring you in the first place."

Ash shook his head. "No, Miss Hart. I don't mean I see them artistically or in my imagination. I mean, I actually see emotions. In color."

Miss Hart blinked, sitting up a little straighter. "I don't understand."

He spent the next half hour explaining, and finally, understanding dawned upon Miss Hart. "Fascinating," she muttered. Then, after a pause, she tilted her head. "Can I ask—what's my color?"

The question caught Ash off guard, and he hesitated. "Well... I don't actually know what to call your essence."

"Essence?" she echoed.

Ash nodded. "Yeah. I refer to the colors as 'essences.' It makes things easier to understand."

Miss Hart hummed in thought. "And what happened yesterday... is it related to this?"

Ash exhaled deeply. "Yeah. All of a sudden, I can't see them anymore. It just... stopped. And I don't know what that means." His fingers curled into his sleeves. "It feels like missing an arm."

Miss Hart was quiet for a moment, studying him with an unreadable expression. Then, she leaned back slightly, her fingers tapping against the arm of her chair. "I don't think I can truly understand what it's like to lose something like that," she admitted. "But I can share a story—one my grandmother used to tell me."

Ash glanced up, surprised. "A story?"

She nodded. "My grandmother believed that some gifts— especially those tied to the spirit—aren't permanent. She used to say they come and go like the seasons, following their own rhythms that are beyond our understanding."

Ash frowned slightly, intrigued despite himself. "What do you mean?"

Miss Hart smiled, folding her hands in her lap. "When I was little, she told me about a healer in our village—

someone who could ease pain with just a touch. For years, people came to him, desperate for relief, and he never turned them away. But one day, his gift vanished. No reason, no warning. Just gone."

Ash swallowed, a strange sense of familiarity creeping in. "What did he do?"

"At first, he panicked. He felt useless—like he had lost the very thing that defined him. Without his gift, he questioned everything. How could he help people now? Who was he without it?" She paused, watching Ash closely. "But my grandmother said the absence of his gift forced him to see the world differently. He had spent so long relying on that one ability that he had ignored the other ways he could heal. Without it, he listened more. Observed more. He learned how to read people—not just their pain, but their fears, their joys, the things they left unspoken. And when his gift finally returned, it wasn't the same." But my grandmother told me that his gift wasn't truly gone; it was just resting."

Ash hesitated. "How was it different?"

"It was deeper," Miss Hart said. "More refined. Before, he had used it instinctively, but now he understood it. He didn't just take away pain—he helped people carry it and taught them how to heal themselves. Losing his gift was what made him truly grow into it."

Ash frowned. "Resting?"

Miss Hart nodded. "Some abilities aren't meant to be constant. They ebb and flow, appearing when they're needed and fading when it's time to grow in a different way. She always said that spiritual gifts follow the same cycles as nature—sometimes they bloom, sometimes they wither, but they never disappear completely."

Ash stared at her, his mind whirling.

"I don't know if that applies to you," Miss Hart admitted. "But maybe… this isn't the end of your gift. Perhaps it's just changing. Maybe, when it returns, you'll see it in a new way."

Ash wasn't sure what to make of that.

On one hand, it was comforting to think his ability wasn't lost. On the other, it left him uneasy. How was it changing? Would the colors return—brighter, louder, impossible to ignore? Or would they come back as something else entirely, something he wasn't prepared for?

The thought twisted in his stomach. He had spent years learning to live with the essences, filtering through the noise without losing himself. If it came back different—more intense, more unpredictable—what then?

Miss Hart must have noticed his hesitation. "Change can be unsettling, but it doesn't have to be bad."

Ash exhaled. "I just don't know what to expect."

"That's fair," she said.

Miss Hart tapped her fingers against the desk, thoughtful. "But maybe I can help you," she said. "I don't know your ability, and perhaps I never will—but you could try drawing it out. The way you've always seen essence."

Ash blinked. "Draw it?"

"Exactly. You've spent your whole life perceiving emotions as colors—maybe putting them on paper will help you understand what's changing." She tilted her head slightly.

Ash didn't think it through much. He had already made up his mind. If anyone could help him, it was Miss Hart. So he rose from his chair, settled behind a blank canvas, and picked up a set of soft pastel brushes.

At first, it felt awkward. He had always relied on the essences to guide him, never needing to articulate it with words or shapes. But now, with sticks of color smudging his fingers, he began to experiment—soft gradients, blending shades, striving to capture how emotions had once bled into one another.

His initial attempts felt clumsy and wrong. Yet, the more he practiced, the more something clicked. He wasn't simply recreating what he used to see—he was understanding it in a new way. He noticed patterns: how warmth and tension intertwined, how emotions didn't just stand alone but merged and shifted. He could still feel them, even without seeing them.

Maybe Miss Hart had been onto something.

By the time he headed back, Ash had completely removed his glasses. The world felt sharper, a little more raw, but he didn't put them back on. Not yet.

When he reached the school gate, Lily was already waiting for him. She took one look at his face and blinked. "Uh… where are your glasses?"

"I took them off."

She frowned. "Yeah, I can see that. But why?"

Ash hesitated, then shrugged. "I'm trying something."

Lily studied him, clearly unsure whether to push or let it be. Eventually, she sighed. "Alright. Just tell me if something's wrong."

Ash almost smiled—typical Lily.

And then—

A flicker of color.

It was faint, barely there, but he saw it: a soft blue halo around Lily, shifting like quiet ripples in water. The sight sent a jolt through him, his breath catching for half a second.

Not gone. Not lost. But changing.

His fingers curled slightly at his side as he exhaled. Maybe Miss Hart had been right. Maybe his gift was transforming.

Chapter 13: Cultural Threads

It was another day at school, and as always, Ash headed for his extra class with Miss Hart in the art classroom. However, as he opened the door, the first thing he noticed was smoke.

For a split second, his breath caught. Seeing smoke rise from the art room was unusual, especially since Miss Hart didn't smoke. The immediate alarm in his chest made him scan the room, searching for her, ensuring she was safe. But there she was, perfectly fine, moving around with the source of the smoke in her hands: three long, thin pieces of wood, their ends glowing with slow-burning embers.

The wisps of smoke curled into the air, almost weightless, as if they were carrying whispers with them. Ash exhaled, steadying himself, and as he did, he caught the scent: warm, earthy, and faintly sweet. It enveloped him like a well-worn blanket, settling something within him he hadn't realized was restless. In all his time spent in this room, hunched over paper and color, he had never experienced anything like it.

Then he took in the rest of the room. Most of the chairs had been pushed back to create space in the middle. Two seats faced each other, and between them sat a metal cylinder holding more of the same thin burning sticks.

Ash frowned. "What's going on, Miss Hart? You do know we're not allowed to have anything burning in the art class, right? We have flammable stuff in here."

Miss Hart had always been a little unconventional, but that was part of what made her a good teacher—at least in Ash's opinion. She had a way of understanding things beyond just technique or theory. She sensed the weight people carried, the invisible threads that tied them in knots. Maybe that was why Ash trusted her more than most adults.

This, though, was unexpected, even for her.

She looked up when he spoke, a small smile tugging at her lips. "Oh, you're here, Ash."

Then, as if he hadn't just pointed out the apparent fire hazard, she waved a hand dismissively. "Don't worry about it. I cleared out all the flammable stuff for our session today, and I already told the principal, so I have permission."

Ash watched as she carefully placed the burning wood in the metal cylinder between them.

"Come on in," Miss Hart said, patting the empty seat across from her. "Close the door. I have something special for you today."

Ash hesitated for only a second before stepping inside, shutting the door behind him with a quiet click. He moved toward the seat, lowering himself onto it with slight awkwardness, crossing his legs as best as he could.

He looked at her expectantly. "What's next?"

Miss Hart studied him for a moment. "Are you still struggling with seeing the essences?"

Ash sighed, running a hand through his hair. "Yeah. I can see them a little, but it's been pretty dull going for a while."

She nodded as if she had anticipated that answer. "I don't know if this will help, but my grandmother taught me a trick for when my head was clouded with too much noise—too many thoughts and emotions that weren't mine. It helped me regain focus, to separate what was real from the background static."

Ash tilted his head slightly, intrigued despite himself. "And the burning wood?"

Miss Hart's smile widened a little. "It's sage. People have used it for centuries to clear out old energy and make space for something new. I thought it might help you see more clearly."

Ash stared at the smoke drifting lazily through the air, the scent wrapping around him. Although the smell was intense, it was far from uncomfortable. In fact, as he took a slow breath, Ash felt the most at ease he had in a while.

"Okay," he said. "I'm listening."

Miss Hart smiled, her hands resting on her knees as she settled into a relaxed posture. "Do you remember when I taught you about 'los que sienten'?"

Ash nodded, and Miss Hart continued, "My grandmother was one of them," she said. "In our culture, these were the people who could sense the emotional weather of their communities, the ones who could read the residue left behind in spaces and people."

Ash straightened slightly, intrigued.

Miss Hart let her gaze drift to the smoke curling toward the ceiling. "It wasn't just about feeling what others felt—it was about understanding the weight emotions leave behind, how places can hold onto grief, and how rooms can remember laughter. The elders used to say that spaces with heavy energy needed to be cleared to make room for renewal. That's why they burned herbs like sage and palo santo. Not just as a ritual, but as a way to reset what lingers."

Ash exhaled, watching the wisps of smoke shift with his breath. That concept resonated in a way that was difficult to articulate. He had always sensed something in different spaces—some rooms felt like open wounds, while others resembled faded photographs of warmth long gone. It wasn't just about people; it was in places, too.

Miss Hart gestured for him to sit more comfortably. "Let's try something," she said. "Meditation isn't about forcing your mind to be still; it's about giving it space to sort through what's there. We'll start with breathing."

Ash nodded and shifted into a more relaxed position. Miss Hart's voice was steady and warm as she guided him. "Close your eyes. Breathe in through your nose for four seconds... hold it for four... now exhale through your mouth for six."

He followed her lead, the rhythm unfamiliar at first. His breaths had always been reactionary—shortened when overwhelmed and held when anxious. But this was a little more challenging than he'd anticipated. It was difficult to hold his breath deliberately.

Miss Hart continued, "Focus on the way the air moves through you. Let it settle in your chest, then release it. Each breath clears out the clutter, like waves smoothing over the sand."

Ash allowed himself to sink into the feeling. The tension in his shoulders eased, and his usually buzzing mind quieted just a little. The smoke still curled in the air, its scent grounding him. He hadn't realized how much weight he had been carrying until it started to lift.

After a few more cycles, Miss Hart let the silence settle before speaking again. "How do you feel?"

Ash opened his eyes slowly. "Better," he admitted. He hadn't even noticed when the tightness in his chest had dissipated.

Miss Hart smiled. "Good. Meditation helps clear out what lingers, just like the smoke does. It's not about getting rid of feelings; it's about making space for them to exist without overwhelming you."

Ash nodded, but as he did, his mind drifted back home to his mother. She carried so much, and maybe… maybe something like this could help her too. Hesitating, he asked,

"Miss Hart, can you teach me how to do this at home? How do you guide someone else through it?"

Miss Hart's expression softened, but there was a cautious look in her eyes. "You're still too young, Ash, to guide someone else through meditation techniques," she said gently. "It might look easy, but navigating someone through their most chaotic memories and clearing them out is dangerous."

Ash frowned slightly. "But—"

She raised a hand before he could protest. "How about this? Instead of leading someone else, you practice it for yourself first. Focus on simple yoga and breathing exercises. Learn how to ground yourself before you try to help others."

He wanted to argue, but deep down, he knew she was right. He wasn't ready for that kind of responsibility yet. So he nodded. "Alright."

***

For the next few weeks, their sessions became a quiet rhythm, with smoke curling through the air, slow and steady breaths, and conversations stretching between them like invisible threads. Miss Hart taught him how to sit with his thoughts rather than push them away and how to let his mind settle instead of wrestling with emotions that weren't always his own.

One afternoon, as they sat cross-legged on the floor, Ash let out a deep breath, his eyes half-lidded from the stillness. Then, curiosity broke through the calm. "Miss Hart," he asked, "when you said your grandmother taught you these things… what did you mean?"

A small smile tugged at the corners of her lips as she set down the bundle of sage in her hands. "My grandmother could walk into a space and sense everything weighing on the people inside. She always said it was like standing in a storm and knowing which way the wind would blow before it even moved."

Ash frowned slightly. "That sounds… familiar."

"I thought it might," Miss Hart replied, studying him for a moment before continuing. "People like my grandmother—like you—were seen as essential to the community's balance. They could sense what others carried, even when it wasn't spoken aloud. Sometimes, they helped clear out emotions that lingered too long in places and people."

Ash hesitated before asking, "Is that why you believe me so easily? Most people would think I was making it up."

Miss Hart nodded. "Yes. I grew up hearing stories and watching my grandmother work. She taught me that healing isn't solely about the physical—it's about the weight we carry. In both Native traditions and my own Mexican heritage, cleansing isn't superstition. It's about clearing space, making room for something lighter. Everything I've learned is meant to help realign people with themselves."

Ash let out a slow breath, his gaze fixed on the smoke swirling between them. "Miss Hart, I still struggle to see the essence." He looked up at her, frustration creeping into his voice. "Wasn't this session supposed to help me see it again? I still don't understand how this is supposed to work."

Miss Hart met his gaze, calm and steady. "Ash, you've misunderstood. This isn't about the others at all."

He frowned. "What do you mean?"

"The reason you can't see essence right now isn't something outside of you—it's something within you."

Ash sighed, running a hand through his hair. "Yeah, I know. Last time, you said it was evolving."

Miss Hart smiled, tilting her head. "It could be. That's one possibility. But it's not the only one."

He squinted at her. "What do you mean?"

She leaned forward slightly. "This practice isn't about forcing your ability back—it's about clearing your mind. Letting go of the things that weigh you down, the thoughts that pull you in too many directions at once. Imagine your mind is covered in a thick, stormy cloud. If that cloud is swirling with unnecessary noise, how can you possibly see beyond it?"

Ash exhaled, considering her words. "I can't. Not unless I clear it up first."

Miss Hart nodded. "Exactly."

Something settled in his chest—an understanding that wasn't immediate but was there, waiting to take root.

Then, with a stretch, Miss Hart stood up and dusted off her jeans. "Alright. Stand up and get ready for the next part of our session."

Ash stood, stretching out his legs as Miss Hart moved toward the far side of the room, where she had set up a different workspace. Unlike their usual supplies—charcoal, pastels, and acrylics—this table held something different: sheets of handmade paper, natural pigments in small ceramic dishes, and delicate brushes that looked worn with years of use.

Miss Hart gestured for him to sit. "Today, we're doing something a little different."

Ash raised a brow. "Different, how?"

Miss Hart picked up one of the brushes, rolling it between her fingers. "Art isn't just about expression—it's about connection. Every tradition has its own way of using art to process emotions, to make sense of the intangible."

Ash glanced at the materials, hesitant. "I don't exactly have the best track record with traditional art."

Miss Hart chuckled softly. "That's not the point. This isn't about skill; it's about the process." She dipped the brush into one of the pigments—a deep, earthy red—and dragged it across the paper in a single, deliberate stroke. "In Mexican and Native traditions, colors carry meaning. This red, for example? It represents the heart, the root of emotion. When we paint with it, we focus on what grounds us."

Ash reached for a brush, mimicking her movements. As he laid down his own stroke of red, she continued, "We also have black—linked to introspection, to the unseen. Gold and yellow? They carry light, clarity." She handed him another dish, this one filled with a muted, ochre-like shade. "For this exercise, you're not painting an image. You're painting what you feel. Don't think too much—just let it happen."

He frowned but dipped his brush into the yellow anyway, adding uneven streaks over the red. He expected it to feel forced, but as he worked, something shifted. The act of moving the brush, of blending color into color, had a rhythm to it—one that bypassed the tangled mess in his mind.

Miss Hart watched him for a moment before speaking again. "Another technique my grandmother used was carving. Sometimes, when emotions feel too big, it helps to work with something solid. Clay, wood, even stone." She pulled out a small block of soft clay. "Have you ever tried working with this?"

Ash shook his head.

Miss Hart pressed her thumb into the clay, shaping it without overthinking. "It's tactile. Grounding. When you shape something with your hands, it pulls you into the present. It helps clear away the noise." She pushed the clay toward him. "Go on."

He hesitated before pressing his fingers into the cool surface. The material was oddly soothing. He didn't know what he was making—he wasn't even trying to create anything specific—but the simple act of shaping, of molding, quieted something restless inside him.

Miss Hart leaned back, allowing him to work in silence for a while before speaking again.

Ash remained quiet as his fingers moved instinctively, pressing and shaping, smoothing out edges before reshaping them. He didn't have an image in mind—only a feeling. The clay took form slowly, his hands working through the silence until, without realizing it, he had created something familiar—a small, rectangular block with softened edges, just slightly curved—a notebook.

He stared at it, his chest tightening.

Miss Hart tilted her head, observing. "A notebook," she murmured. "Are you worried about exams, perhaps?"

Ash shook his head. "No." The word was quiet, almost absentminded. His fingers traced the ridges where the pages would be.

A memory surfaced—Addie's notebook, the worn cover, and the familiar drawings. The weight of it in his hands that day. He swallowed hard.

"I think I'm guilty, Miss Hart."

She didn't react right away. She simply sat with his words, giving them space. "I don't know what you're guilty about," she eventually said, her voice steady and measured. "And I won't ask. But I hope you can rise above it."

Ash clenched his jaw.

"Guilt can be a very deadly poison," she continued gently. "It lingers, seeps into everything, and makes you carry weight that isn't always yours to bear. Sometimes, we fall into that pit over the smallest things—things that may not even be as heavy as we think."

He exhaled slowly, his eyes fixed on the small clay notebook.

"That's why," Miss Hart said softly, "I hope you can clear it up with the person you feel guilty about. Okay?"

Ash nodded. "Okay."

Epilogue

Exams were drawing near, and Ash had thrown himself into studying day and night. Even Lily, his sister, had become preoccupied with preparations, and the entire energy at school had shifted. The air thrummed with tension—nervous, restless, and on the verge of snapping under the weight of looming deadlines.

Consequently, Ash's ability to see essence had returned with a vengeance. Everywhere he looked, his head throbbed, and his ears rang. The classrooms, the hallways, the restrooms, even the cafeteria, the art room, the backyard, and the front yard—there was no escape. The sheer number of students, each radiating their own tangled emotions, had created an overwhelming, writhing mass of energy.

Blobs of stress clung to their hosts in thick, murky swirls. Some dripped with sluggish exhaustion, and others crackled with sharp, erratic fear. The worst were those that flickered with quiet, contained desperation—the kind that hid behind calm faces but whispered of sleepless nights and clenched fists beneath desks.

There were only two places he could study: his room at home and the dark, vacant corner of the school library.

He had claimed a small, dust-covered desk at the back, wedged between rows of outdated encyclopedias and forgotten archives. No one else ever came here, and for that, he was grateful. The dim lighting cast long shadows across the pages of his books, and the silence was thick enough to muffle the restless murmurs beyond the library walls. Here, the chaotic swirl of emotions dulled to a faint hum, distant enough that he could finally think. But even here, his mind wasn't entirely at peace.

The clay notebook still sat untouched on his desk at home, its presence a quiet weight pressing against his thoughts. He didn't know what to do with it. Every time he looked at it, something in his chest tightened—like a breath held too long. He should have reached out to her by now. He knew that. But he was afraid of what he would find. Guilt tangled around him like thorned vines, and every time he thought about it, he found a reason to push it aside.

So, instead, he buried himself in equations and essays, in historical dates and biological diagrams. If he exhausted himself, he wouldn't have to think. If he drowned in coursework, he wouldn't have to face what was eating at him. It wasn't the best plan, but it worked—at least until he heard a pair of erratic steps and an unusually familiar, heavy breathing.

Ash stood up from his chair, his pulse quickening as he peered around the nearest bookshelf. The sound had come, from just beyond the rows of forgotten encyclopedias, where the dim lighting barely reached. He found himself staring at a male student hunched over a desk, his hands gripping the edges so tightly his knuckles had turned white.

His essence was a storm barely contained. Fear, dread, helplessness, stress, anxiety—all tangled into a single, writing mass, forming a color Ash had only recently come to recognize. The distinct, sharp-edged shade of a panic attack.

The boy was whispering to himself, voice trembling. "I can do it. I can do it. I can—" His breath hitched, his shoulders rising and falling too fast. His body tensed like a bowstring pulled too tight, moments from snapping.

Then, suddenly—

"I can't. I can't. I can't—" His voice broke, and with it, his composure. His gasping breaths turned ragged, hands shaking as he gripped his hair. His entire form curled inward as if trying to disappear into himself.

Ash stiffened.

He knew this. He had lived through this. Not long ago, he had sat at a desk in this very library, trapped in the same spiral, his mind caving in under the weight of pressure and panic. He had felt the same crushing helplessness, the world closing in, leaving no way out—until Addie came along.

She had reached for him, grounded him in a way he hadn't known he needed. And now, here was someone else caught in the same relentless current, sinking fast.

For a moment, Ash hesitated. But before he could talk himself out of it, he stepped forward. Moving cautiously, he crouched down so he wouldn't loom over the student. His voice was soft, careful.

"Hey."

The boy flinched at the sound, his breath coming in sharp, uneven gasps.

Ash raised his hands in a gesture of peace. "Please don't be alarmed. I just want to help. Can I?"

For a moment, there was no response—just the frantic rise and fall of the boy's chest. Then, slowly, he gave a shaky nod.

Ash reached out, his grip gentle as he guided the student to sit on the ground. "Come on, don't fight it. Close your eyes and just breathe. Hold it in—then let it out."

The boy struggled, his lungs still locked in a desperate rhythm, but Ash stayed with him, unwavering.

"It's easy to feel buried under everything," Ash said, keeping his voice low. "Exams, friends, family... Sometimes, it all crumbles at once, and suddenly, you're sinking—like you're deep underwater, and the weight of the world is pressing down on you." He exhaled slowly. "But what if you saw it differently? You're not drowning. You're diving. Down into the deep blue sea, where endless possibilities are waiting."

The boy's trembling had eased, and Ash felt he should stop here. But something within him wanted to go on.

"I understand you," Ash continued, his chest tightening. Memories surfaced unbidden, but he didn't push them away. "You feel alone, like no one sees you. Like no one cares." He hesitated. "The world feels dark. Unforgiving. You just want space to breathe, to be yourself—but the people around you don't make it easy. And after a while, the weight of it all… it drains you until you feel empty. Like your flame's been snuffed out."

A strangled noise tore from the boy's throat. His hands clenched into fists, his breathing turning erratic again—but this time, it wasn't panic. It was something else.

Upon opening his eyes, Ash was met with something new—something sharp and electric, crackling in the air between them. It wasn't just fear. It wasn't just distress. It was an essence, raw and unfiltered, directed solely at him.

Then, in a sudden burst of motion, the student tore away from him, scrambling to his feet. His breaths came fast and shallow, his entire frame shaking as he backed away.

"Freak," he choked out, his voice barely above a whisper—hoarse, terrified.

Ash flinched as if the word had struck him.

The boy didn't wait for a response. He turned and bolted, his footsteps pounding against the floor, echoing in the empty hallway.

Meanwhile, Ash remained frozen in place, still kneeling, still reaching for something that had already slipped through his fingers. His heart pounded, his pulse thrumming in his ears, drowning out everything else.

He had tried to help. He had meant to pull the student back from the edge, to steady him. Instead, he had driven him away.

The realization settled in his chest like a heavy stone.

What had he done?

Even though Miss Hart had told him not to lead anyone through meditation yet, he had. And now, he had gone and made things worse.

A faint tremor ran through his fingers—he needed to see Miss Hart.

Ash gathered his things with clumsy hands, shoving his books into his bag without care. The library's silence pressed in around him, thick and stifling. He put on his headphones and glasses before he got out of there.

By the time he reached the faculty offices, his pulse had steadied, but his nerves had not. He hesitated in the hallway, staring at Miss Hart's closed door. Then, before he could second-guess himself, he knocked.

But there was no answer.

He frowned. Maybe she was in class? Or maybe—

"Looking for Miss Hart?"

Ash turned sharply. Marcus came from across the hallway, "She's not here."

Ash's stomach tightened. "Do you know when she'll be back?"

Marcus hesitated, and that was the first sign that something was wrong. "Uh… she transferred."

Ash blinked. "What?"

"Yeah. Family emergency. She left a few days ago. Pretty sudden." Marcus shrugged, "No one really knows if she's coming back."

The words struck Ash like a physical blow.

Gone? Miss Hart was *gone?*

He stood there, frozen, as the gravity of the news settled on him. The one teacher who had seen him—who had recognized his struggles, who had guided him through them—was suddenly, inexplicably gone. And no one had told him.

He tried to swallow past the lump in his throat, but his voice still came out unsteady. "Did… did she leave anything? A note? Anything at all?"

Marcus shook his head. "Not that I know of." He glanced at Ash then, frowning slightly. "You okay?"

He wasn't but nodded anyway. "Yeah. Thanks," he said, turning before Marcus could press further, walking away on autopilot. His mind felt hollow, his body weightless. It wasn't just Miss Hart leaving. It was what it *meant.*

She had been a tether—one of the only people who had understood what he was going through, who had never made him feel like a burden, who had given him hope that he could manage this… whatever this was.

Now, she was gone.

And Ash was alone.

He reached the nearest stairwell and stopped. The distant hum of students in the hallways blurred into white noise. His hands felt numb, his breath was too shallow, and his chest—

No.

He pressed a hand to his sternum, grounding himself. He couldn't fall apart here. He had to move.

But it had been a long time since he felt he had nowhere to go.

Author's Note

We hope you found this book useful. If you have any questions or feedback, please reach out to me at lynn@thecolorofmelancholy.com

You can also visit our website for additional resources and information, to order more copies of the book, etc., at www.thecolorofmelancholy.com.

Look forward to additional volumes of this text in the near future. You can find more information on the website above and preorder copies.

Thank you.